A Skin Diary

Poetry
Fairground Music
The Tree that Walked
Cannibals and Missionaries
Epistles to Several Persons
The Mountain in the Sea
Lies and Secrets
The Illusionists
Waiting for the Music
The Beautiful Inventions
Selected Poems 1954 to 1982
Partingtime Hall *(with James Fenton)*
The Grey Among the Green
The Mechanical Body
Stones and Fires
Collected Poems

Fiction
Flying to Nowhere
The Adventures of Speedfall
Tell It Me Again
The Burning Boys
Look Twice
The Worm and the Star

Criticism
A Reader's Guide to W.H. Auden
The Sonnet

For Children
Herod Do Your Worst
Squeaking Crust
The Spider Monkey Uncle King
The Last Bid
The Extraordinary Wool Mill and other stories
Come Aboard and Sail Away

Edited
The Chatto Book of Love Poetry
The Dramatic Works of John Gay

A Skin Diary

John Fuller

Chatto & Windus
LONDON

First published in 1997

1 3 5 7 9 10 8 6 4 2

Copyright © 1997 by John Fuller

John Fuller has asserted his right under
the Copyright, Designs and Patents Act, 1988
to be identified as the author of this work

First published in Great Britain in 1997 by
Chatto & Windus Limited
Random House, 20 Vauxhall Bridge Road
London SW1V 2SA

Random House Australia (Pty) Limited
20 Alfred Street, Milsons Point, Sydney
New South Wales 2061, Australia

Random House New Zealand Limited
18 Poland Road, Glenfield
Auckland 10, New Zealand

Random House South Africa (Pty) Limited
PO Box 337, Bergvlei, South Africa

Random House UK Limited Reg. No. 954009

Papers used by Random House UK Limited are natural, recyclable
products made from wood grown in sustainable forests. The
manufacturing processes conform to the environmental regulations of
the country of origin

A CIP catalogue record for this book
is available from the British Library

ISBN: 0 7011 6669 X

Typeset by Palimpsest Book Production Limited
Polmont, Stirlingshire
Printed and bound in Great Britain by
Mackay's of Chatham, PLC, Chatham, Kent

Dedication

For Sophie, Louisa and Emily

Imagination's a game
Where we wish to entertain
A past (or a future) unknown:

Here are familiar mountains,
The imagined lives they contain
And some of their secrets shown.

We have stood by the ferns of their fire
That nod a little in rain
And looked at their sky from stone

And silently vowed (as I do
With you on this page once again)
That we fully imagine our own.

Becoming is something of a mystery. At first there is simply nothing, an emptiness without shape. But nothing comes of nothing. You know that, don't you. And what you should also know, though you do not know it, is that two things become another thing. This thing out here, like a boy at the window searching for his shadow, needs the two other things to come together in secret to give him a chance. And there you are! And here, therefore, am I. And it.

But you know nothing about it, funny thing that it is.

And what would *he*, Gruffudd, say about it?

In the beginning was the worm?

Or would he say it was a flight of fancy? Idle talk, gossip, speculation and rumour? A false alarm? A nine months' wonder? A nonentity, a cipher, a no-name?

Call it anything and you begin to know where you are. 'I am what you have expected all your life. I am so familiar that you have quite forgotten what I am. Now you will have to name me again.'

And he? He knows even less.

Sunday 19 April

You notice some part of yourself as if for the first time, some locus of nail or knuckle that now has a message for the travelling eye. But there is nothing to tell. Nothing to know, and nothing to say if you knew. After all, it might not happen. But the journey has begun. And I, who have existed for so long, for just as ever so long as your eyes caught glimpses of me in the shadow of his amber eyes, I know it. I know that the two things have become one thing, like the arch between pillars.

I never had a body before. It's like Christmas, a long excitement, a speculation, an opening. It's an idea given a future. It's the perpetually pre-existent given its present. Hurrah!

It's eternity realised, like a paper profit you've no idea how to spend. It's the heart of things, the twisted cradle-strings of two pairs of eyes and the shape that's made between them, flowers of flesh like the brief blooms in fire.

It's a resurrection the size of a pin-head.

Monday 20 April

As you dust down your body, the only perfection is the unimagined. And isn't the unimagined your sense of what you should be imagining? It is like an anointing, a sacrifice, when the announcement of the blood calls for a male without blemish. Not you, not only you, but another. These surfaces of skin unpopulated.

And the vials stand in order, rose and kohl, turtledoves and young pigeons, skin food and astringents, stoppered milks and feathers in powder.

And above the steam it is clouds of snow in blossom, a sweet savour falling on an inviolate altar. A girl's body, with moles in peculiar places.

And the offering has begun its journey, the trickling tributaries.

Tuesday 21 April

Today, apparently by chance, you remember how just over a week ago the little boys of the village came round with their wooden clappers, asking for eggs:

'Clap, clap, gofyn wy, i hogia' bach ar y plwy!' It was the Monday before Easter, and Twm and all the boys of the parish wanted eggs. Little wriggly boys! Catch them by their tails and they'd half wriggle out of their trousers! You wondered if their seeds would wriggle out as easily if you were to catch them by their jimmies, popping them out happily like shelling a pea-pod.

An egg has more substance, doesn't it? It's complete and actual, and it stays where it is.

Until its cover is blown. Then its jellies gather and tremble at the pin-hole and drift into sticky lost strands.

The little boys blowing away the matter, as the stars are blown away, and it might as well be seeds for all the chances that it has.

Clap, clap! And it takes its colours like the shell of the thing it will be.

Wednesday 22 April

Call it a visitant and right away you make it much more willed, as though you've launched into a story, with motives to come, and dramatic moments of self-identification. 'I have come to make you suffer!' You might be able to squeeze an explanation out of that, eventually.

But to you it will seem arbitrary, something that might not have happened.

And on the dresser are all the painted egg-faces you made in their delicate expressions and colours: saffron mandarin smiles, pencilled frowns, goofy onionskin yokels with cracked pates. And the one you did with Gruffudd from the vermilion lozenge in the black enamelled tin with the overlapping lids, itself like a medical specimen-box or monstrance for the crusted or welling shades of shed blood, umber, madder, carmine. The one that linked two hearts, swelling with the shell.

It was like a little house to be inhabited, a land to be possessed, that empty egg.

Thursday 23 April

Already your mother and father are talking of marriage.
But they are talking about it anyway. It seems to be the
state of things, the heart of the matter. You admit nothing
and you deny nothing, but sit between them, thinking of
all your friends who have married: pale Hefyd Hughes
who rolled down her stockings to show her veins, little
blue scribbles on the calves like the way the river runs
through Tanwy; Megan from the bakery, who took to
wearing hats with dead birds in them; Polly Parry, who
stopped laughing.

You know it must be serious, a very serious matter
indeed if it takes you nearer death like that, compulsive
like a reaching hand in a dark cavern. They say that they
like him, too, knowing all the time you spend in your
room and the smell of your room when you've been in
it, like the flower tent at the Easter Show, Twm said.
Really, they would like to know how things stand.
They are looking at the lie of the land, the footing of
it. They are conjecturing the conjuncture, its suitability,
its convenience. And often they do it with a twinkle that
makes you blush and snap.

And all the time your clasped hands are not an inch
from where the ark of the covenant passes clean over
Jordan.

Friday 24 April

So what is the situation? The two things have become one thing, which excludes everything else and invites no comparisons. There were harbingers and intimations, perhaps, but no instructions. As long as they were two, the hero could not fail because he could not act. Now, everything is potential, the trumpet raised to the lips. The stage entrance is lit.

Did you see the curate with his pomegranate? The wonder at its fullness, just space enough and no more for every jellied cell? You can't tell how many there are unless you open it and count.

Did you expect him to come tonight? Did your mother lay out the cloth with the Egyptian markings? And were you sick this morning, and did you put it out of your mind?

Saturday 25 April

Separation is over (did you think it had just begun?) and relationship is the order of the day (perhaps you thought it had ended?).

I have a sense that everything is related. For example: the wall behind the stove meets the inner walls of the chimney-piece and the chimney beam has to those walls the relation of connection, forming a bridge above their frontal planes. Another example: the deep onion smell

6

from the pot on the stove reaches your father's nose, which must be related to his hand, for his hand puts down his newspaper in order to lift the lid of the pot so that the same smell can rise unimpeded.

Perhaps Gruffudd will come tonight, though he is not expected.

Sunday 26 April

In Saron today, there he is! And there is everybody, too, converging upon the temple of the Lord in their twos and threes as if to contribute a soul for each stone, as if to re-enact the building of the temple. You look towards him for a sign.

But for a sign of what? You've no idea, and he doesn't know either. You know nothing of it, and he knows nothing of it. He in his containment, his quiet interrogation, expecting nothing; you in your uncertainty, your unassuming silence, expecting everything. The dust rises from the pulpit under the blows of the sermon.

And all the time it is dividing, breaking, settling in. It is harboured now. It is lodged. It is attendant in its temple, awaiting the word.

Monday 27 April

If there is one thing there must be another. Your father raises his axe, slowly, like an iron flag of victory. It descends. The spoils are divided. The inner faces of the log falling to the left and the right, inverted contours of each other, secret and clean. He kicks them together and places another log on the step. The axe rises. And falls.

But the true symmetry belonged to the tree, from the twin leaves of the seedling to the matched ache of root and branch. It is a symmetry you now share. In feature, and in cell.

In the beginning was the axe.

'We can't be letting the stove go out, can we?'

Tuesday 28 April

You are much more like your mother than your father. Her energy reaches out to all corners of the house, as her arms reach out to smooth the edges of the tablecloth. It radiates from a centre.

What feeds that centre? What prevents it from ever being extinguished?

Since you are so like her, you must know. But you give no thought to it. You look in the looking glass at the straight nose and the wave in the hair and if you think of it at all it is like copying a drawing. Or tracing over with sharp pencil, breathing carefully, following the line through the cake-lining paper, dim as reeds trapped beneath the ice of ponds. 'She's got your nose.'

And your father, reaching over to you with his thumb wiggling between his first two fingers: 'No! *I've* got it!'

And your mother, only this morning: 'Who ate all the cheese?' You know it wasn't your father, but you think no more of it.

And what about it itself, that will wiggle enough in time? You give no thought to it either. But it is no illusion.

Wednesday 29 April

They go together, though. Like the kiss and the hurt finger, like the silence and the echo, like the whip and the clown, like the trust and the satisfaction, like the elbow and the stomach, like the rebuke and the smile, like the stove and the tree.

Your parents define the compatible, for you would hardly know if they were not. They are the intersecting dimensions that create your space, the alternating orbits that rule your day and night. Your own life could only be a conscious departure from their constitution, an obvious variation of the established model. Your trajectory conforms to their axes, your journeys can only depart from their harbour. You know nothing else.

And it knows nothing of that, as yet. Although it is already collecting the information.

Thursday 30 April

What is the blood doing? Just when you expect it to put in an appearance it is off somewhere in secret making bargains with the intruder.

And where is he, then? Where is Gruffudd? Sometimes he is there and sometimes not.

But he left his calling card, didn't he?

I didn't want to make that joke. It brings awkward images of him to mind, buttoned up and shining for that Sunday visit that he never made, the one that now he must make to them as much as to you, to them much more than to you, with his cap folded in on itself in his working hands like a pasty and the great apple of guilt in his throat, stealing their daughter and asking for their approval.

Tongue-tied at the door, on his best behaviour.

Friday 1 May

That's the other great hinge of relation. The woman like a doorway, the man like the door. The one is always a welcome, the other a demurral.

You can work out which is which.

One is inevitably a passage from one state to another, the other a barrier. One is the defining shape of transit, an invitation. The other is precisely the shape of completion, an urge to acceptance. One is darkness, the other substance. One is immutable, the other stands askance: its strengthening bars are the Zs of its repose. Its latch stands proud, but withdraws just at the moment of engagement. It shadows the threshold.

It is the hinge that bears the weight of expectation. Who knows if it is the door or the doorway that sets up such a wailing and a creaking?

The pin is already in place, and will neither move nor be still.

Saturday 2 May

It needs no prophet to tell of that instinct of the light which is a new life. They must see it on your forehead, radiating like a crown of stars, like the spokes of the driven chariot of your knowledge. For now you do know. You know all that there is to know of the great change that haunts your future. You know it in the cease of blood and the hoarding of flowers. You know it in the way that the blood itself knows it. It is sorrow that can't long be sorrow. It is joy that has a long journey before it can become joy.

You see it in Taid's eyes at Saturday tea, alive on you in a kind of wonder, far from understanding what it is that so contents him under the May blossom and the froth of racing clouds, taking your arm afterwards out through the garden.

Now lettest thou thy servant depart in peace.

Sunday 3 May

Up the spout? Is it true? And might they send you packing? For such a little thing? Really the biggest thing, the only thing, the thing that you are yourself, after all? Everything out there just for you and no one else? The great illusion?

This one not-so-little thing would be the conclusive piece of evidence to disprove the illusion. You say you are the only consciousness in the universe, an untrustful onlooker in your personal theatre of deception, the victimised centre of contrived accidents? Are you so? Can you be so? And eat so much cheese?

Mair, Mair, did you do all this by yourself?

Monday 4 May

I'm beginning to see what it's up to. You have to respect it, three layers of skin and only the improvident would think of belt-and-braces. Something you thought you'd missed and it turns out to have a life of its own.

But now you are running down the hill with the wind at your back. It's as though it is urging you on to the encounter, summoning your determination. And your thoughts are mocked by a swirling school of crows, making another pattern of the wind above you as though it, and you, had two minds.

At Hendre-nant, Mrs Price greets you in that way

of hers that doesn't tell you whether you are somehow expected or a complete surprise. Her eyes settle on yours as she wipes her hands on her apron, and you've no idea whether you are the embodiment of her secret fear and obsession or simply of no account at all.

You long for at least the amiable mask put on for strangers, the polite smile or greeting. Not this soulless recognition, not this wariness. There is no intimacy in it, though that must be its excuse. For without a word from you, she tells you that Gruffudd has taken the trap into town and won't be back until the afternoon. And she stands at the doorway, as if there were some small courtesy belonging to pity, until you have gone.

You would like to take her by the shoulders and shake her until the hairpins bounce off the tiles.

Tuesday 5 May

The son's greatest betrayal is by his mother when he leaves her house, for she sees this act as a betrayal of her. How could it be otherwise? And his sons, and his sons' sons. Her sorrow is not only at his going, but at her betrayal. She gave him life and now has given him over to his own life – giving that can only end in death. It is a kind of Judas kiss, the pain of sewing on his shadow.

Once he was the little bird broken out of the egg, but he can't be a single thing for ever. Youth and joy must unite, the conspiracy of two against one.

This is what your body tells you, Mair, this is what drives you as you seek out Gruffudd day after day. Once again you are striding up the hill. You keep your pace, furious in your lifted skirts, by walking from side to side to make the climb less steep. From a distance it almost looks as though you are moving to avoid the skirling crows in your concentrated, demented zig-zag.

Wednesday 6 May

It strikes a chord. The composition already has some shape. You could begin to tell the head from the tail of it.

You pass a lamb that the crows caught, its body half a memory now, reversing the process. A sprawl of wool on the grass, an exposed backbone, splayed limbs, a little crucifixion. You have seen such a thing many times, but have never thought of it so much in terms of the making and the sorrow of the unmaking.

Think of lambs mobbing a crow!

Thursday 7 May

And the sixth sorrow is knowing that the unmasking must be completed. The finishing is the only thing that is ever finished with. It is the making that goes on for ever.

Where is Uncle Evan who took his harp to cast a spell on Boney? Where is Little Bell the Lost? Where is Tammy? And Arthur Half-way? Where is Idwal who drank the bowl of starch in the larder? Where is Cousin Owen who kissed you on Palm Sunday? Where is Mr Parry, kicked by his mare? Where are the fingers that made the shilling walk? Where is the weeping eye? Where are the white feet pulled with their wool creases out of muddy boots, the toes as surprising as brazil nuts at Christmas?

The made are all unmade. The list is never complete.

Friday 8 May

Something like a mouth and something like an anus, a polarity. One reaches upwards to the air, the other downwards to the earth. The earth is mastered by the earth, a contented cycle. But the air lifts up the syllable and the idea that voyages in it, even though there is nowhere on earth it can go to.

And in the end everything is lifted down and laid on the earth, while the idea of it goes restlessly about searching for a heart that can feel it.

Is this what memory is, that you carve on polished granite to remind yourselves of the endlessness of it, er serchog gof? In loving memory. And the early bluebells in glass jars.

Meanwhile the new life is preparing lips to open against ignorance and a sphincter with which to greet the soil, the primitive streak. The whole world will go straight through.

You have it in mind now to memorialise the future by putting your life in order. After all, it may not be true. You haven't heard me say so, and you can't hear me at all. And in any case, why should you believe me if you could? You cannot feel it. It only declares itself as an absence.

But one beginning prompts another. You are going to take everything up and pummel and smooth and remake. The authority is the light in Taid's eyes, and the bounce of the lambs in the field behind Ty-bach. Your mother and father will respect this mystery, as being in the nature of things. It will be a family decision, or if not a decision, a kind of readiness.

You are going to anchor your sheets and nerve your bolster. You are going to turn in the flap of blanket like an envelope and place the pillow like a stamp, fit for the head of a queen. Resolve is like a bed that you must lie in, and if that resolve concerns another, then he must lie in it too. Or else the queen will have his head off in a trice.

Sunday 10 May

What are your priorities?
1. Not to put off making your list of priorities, but to

make it *now*, here in Saron, where, in spite of the intersection of the Infinite in the dimension of the Finite, time does not stand still but moves onwards, like the shaft of sun that at the beginning of the sermon fell upon the parabolic text of Mrs Unwin's bonnet, moved slowly across her burdened shoulders and now illuminates the unfortunate exemplum of Mr Unwin's chin;

2. Never to marry someone like Mr Unwin;
3. But to marry Gruffudd Price as soon as possible, and thenceforth to sit with him in Saron, bathed in attendant rays of sunlight and invisible anthems of heavenly music;
4. To this end, to stop Gruffudd stroking the underside of his moustache with his forefinger in witty disparagement of your ideas and proposals;
5. To go no further than on the Occasion of the Parlour Floor at Hendre-nant;
6. But on the other hand, to establish that an Occasion of that sort is not only far enough, but for the moment too far;
7. But nonetheless, not to let it appear that the latch on the gate of the Gardens of Delight is to remain unlifted;
8. To make peace of some sort with Mrs Price;
9. To allow the Understanding its full unhindered development, like a pricked-out seedling;
10. To attempt to make some sort of sense of priorities 5, 6 and 7.

Monday 11 May

Arrangement requires everything to be brought together into a significant relationship. The parts are ordered, and systematised according to the governing idea. It's a matter of contrived categorisation, a disposition of roles, a marshalling of expectation. And you can just as well begin at the circumference:

'Have they named the day yet, Mrs Hughes?'

Tuesday 12 May

Little smut! Don't rub it, you'll make it sore! Blink twice and you can forget it. Like a bird blown into a tree, a clattering of wings, soon blown out again but setting up such a commotion. Your heart going when he stood so close.

'I can't see it.'

The eyeball rolled up, like a saint in agonised devotion. Waiting in complete trust for the corner of the handkerchief, the peering tilt of his nose, his breath on your chin.

It's not like that at all. Not a drowned midge, lifted on a corner of linen, but the signpost of dynasty.

Wednesday 13 May

It is your cunning, coming again down the hill, to assume where you subsume. You find him at the lower end of the big field, fencing along the edge of the wood with little Edwin. Edwin is crouched grasping the post with both hands, like a tiny child he is about to lift up by the armpits. Gruffudd has both arms raised, like an executioner. The hammer descends, and the dull smack of sound seems to come like an afterthought from the distant curtain of the wood.

A lock of hair is trapped between his cap and glistening forehead. He looks at you with amusement as if he knew that you would come. Little Edwin takes no notice, in terror of witnessing some impropriety. The hammer is downed, its weight crushing a nettle-clump, but Edwin continues to clutch the post as though it might fall over.

And you begin. It works like this, by creating a class, the members of which exclude all awkward alternatives. Thus initially, the class of days this week when you must meet. If Friday is impossible and Saturday too late, then it must be tomorrow. No question that you might never meet. Even his slow grin acknowledges that.

The principle may be infinitely extended. Of first importance is the small class of your possible answers (yes, or no) to his proposal. Is he not quite certain that he has ever actually made such a proposal? He will soon forget it, when he is obliged to consider which of their acquaintance has, and which does not have, any knowledge of their understanding. And to decide what is to be done about telling them.

But this will have to wait until a time when little Edwin is not close by, gawping.

A Skin Diary

You've got every right to expect something from him, and some right to expect everything from him. As much, at any rate, as from your secret soul-trap, that billet-doux, that nodule, that compulsive skin-diarist down there creating scandal. If the one runs true to type, won't the other? The one is, after all, the other. The shaving from the post, the shaken head of the bluebell, black grains the essence of bluebell, the quiet word whispered in a moment of truth.

Still no flowers.

Having begun, then, you know what the end must be. The end is the time when everything else comes after.

What you don't know is what you don't see, the petal curling, the plate saddling, the first sign of serious shape. Something like a splodge, a wink that might still be tiddled, is folding up to show off one end to the other, sucking in stalk for gut and making it quite clear who's the head.

Now the end has really begun.

In an unimaginable world of perfect consciousness you would examine it together. An almost imperceptible, static but busy and continuous performance, a kind of flea Noh.

What if you could hand it back to him now, this dozy mite, this bowed droplet, let it swim back up that span of release, fighting all the way against the joy-spasms that would expel it, until it reached its lodging-place? Would he be coming up the hill for you? Would he, like you, know without knowing? Claim without claiming? Fight for your acknowledgement and concern?

It is already too large to return. It is the end of the beginning.

Saturday 16 May

O vertures over, let the band play on. You kept him off, did you, and now you will have to keep him on? And how many have there been under the excuse of fancy? Two? Three? Four? Five? And now you've caught the fish alive, catching little fishes on the parlour floor. And you keeping him off like the others, blowing hot and cold in case he were not the one. But now you have an idea that the one is not a who, it's a what. The what is a thing and a question. And the what is now not then. Above all it is not a one at all. The what is it. And you.

Not mealy Maelon dropping his sack, who spoke once when you bent over. Not Iolo the Basket who watered your gate when you were twelve. Not Mr Driscoll who asked the way from his horse and kept you awake with his eyes. Not Dafydd Thomas, who followed you for four months. Not the one with the hair of straw, the nameless angel you had never seen before or since, who passed on the other side of the hawthorn hedge, singing his warning to quiet girls who canoodle:

> 'Gocheled pob merch dawel
> Wrth wasgu a nesu yn isel,
> I lencyn ar ei drafel
> Roi, dan ei bogel, big . . .'

Nor even Gruffudd Price, a shy and humorous man, who certainly wants to marry you, and who, if he has not quite made the proposal, can certainly now be encouraged to do so.

Sunday 17 May

Thinking what it would be like to be two, you don't quite realise that you are already two.

But this week he is in Saron. Looking across to the capel meibion, where the men sit in unusual closeness to each other, without drink, you see an angle of his shaven cheek and ear that is not only bright with soap but bright with the consciousness of being looked at, for he knows where you are sitting as a shepherd knows the evening star.

And when you are married you will sit together in the front pews and you will wear a bonnet like Mrs Unwin. You will walk to the gate with your arms linked as neatly as a puzzle-ring, yours in his like the shaft of the trap, ready to be trotted to a mysterious destiny with your whole life like luggage strapped on.

Afterwards, he tells you (not for the first time) that his cousins had wanted him at the hafod for the summer pasture, but that he had said that he would not go. Does he want you to ask him again why not? Does he want you to say: 'Go, then, if you wish'?

Because you will not say so. There is another light in your eyes that looks out at him, and this time you will not say nothing.

Seeing you together in your serious clothes, talking at a serious distance, close but not too close, like winding off skeins of wool, the question again and again forms itself in the mind and now more often on the tongue:

'Have they named the day yet, Mrs Hughes?'

Monday 18 May

So tonight is the night that he comes, to make the pledge that will seal a family space. For one is a mere point, the centre of our circumference of experience, and two becomes a line, extended like exploration, joining centres, but three are the protecting arms that make the family space.

23

That trilateral space is created out of points of nothingness: single points of location without dimension, self-appointed, radiant but promising a future.

Father, Son and Holy Mother, the triality of nature, three-pointed cell of the human hive, flag of their limitless voyage.

And your father, reaching for his tobacco to be shared and asking all the silly practical questions predicated by his agreement. And Gruffudd smiling, in his Sunday clothes still, and your mother quietly stirring the teapot with the silver spoon.

And it, keeping counsel.

Tuesday 19 May

There's no number where I come from, which is all number and beyond number. The moon has no work to do, but speeds through wisps of cloud with that wincing face of hers.

And now you are beginning to give it a name.

Wednesday 20 May

The grain of wheat is already the whole world, stamped with its promise of growth like the coin of nature. It was, and will be, harvest. Harvest without number.

But trace it to the source, and there is the puzzle indeed. Will the numberless years of broadcast and reaping take you to a beginning? Where is the zero?

It was never told to grow.

Still the sickness. Again and again, waves of it passing through your body, leaving you limp and shaking, a damp curl of hair at your temple like a mark of interrogation.

'Is it really true? Is it this, then, after all?'

Such a small thing still, if you did but know, the grain of wheat. But like a promontory in your body, firm against the tides. Not much now will shake it. You will have to be on terms.

Nothing is unique. No one is alone. All this happened many times before.

Each blade of grass is a signal growth, angled to the sun, look, and a landmark to a looper! It is a struggle, a triumph and a masterstroke.

Think: all flesh is grass, made and mown in a minute. But now you know you will never forget and never be forgotten. You have never looked so closely at the grass before, crispen lanterns, furled flags, bobbing tails, spriggy bits.

Later, you take a bucket of water to the corner of the field so that no one shall come across it and wonder.

Saturday 23 May

Can it go on like this day after day? Yes, of course it can, but soon perhaps the great tides will take it with you, ebbing and flowing, in harmony like the dance at the Plas, his hand in the small of your back, just *there*, guarding if he did but know it the rock on which your tides swirl and sweep. Splayed fingers there like a bridge at billiards and the power of your body surging through them like the waters at Pont Poen. Your hands on his shoulder and arm as if to keep him upright, like a post for hammering.

Soon, yes, the little top-heavy sea-horse will rise and fall with the tide, nodding to a rhythm which you share, a lolling glob, at peace with what you feed it. Of the seven ages of man it is barely on the threshold, but of the wisdom of the seven sages it is the abundant source.

Tell Bias, the past belongs to the whole world, but the future belongs to yourself.

A Skin Diary

No more questions at Saron, only the acknowledgement of understanding, and Twm running in the graves like a mad thing.

You hold the hymns with two flat palms and thumbs in front, like Nain's inlaid music stand. He holds the hymns in his one cupped hand, the other straight down at his side as if it didn't know what it might do or couldn't be controlled but would be away and up with the castrating knife in a trice. Twm is wearing pink dandelions, bloodied, he says, from the leaking corpses in the graves.

Tell Cleobulos, it is no better to be passing out of your life than passing into it.

Monday 25 May

He will buy the ring today, and about time too, for soon it would not be small enough to pass through, like the luck of turning sixpence. Small enough is a kind of blessing as it is.

For already the limbs have budded and suddenly are shaped like paddles, with grooves for fingers, aching to splay in the darkness. This is the day of the moon, but the moon has turned away. Her fences are down, and barren of blood. She has gone to her hafod and herding the stars.

27

Tell Periander, nobody says 'Too early' in the way that they say 'Too late.'

No reason now to join the Pantypistyll Prices at the hafod, but oh the great goose, he busies himself all day with the work that would have given him a good excuse not to go. Can't you hear him saying, as though there were anyone to listen, 'It's these walls want building up, isn't it?' And these walls have been down since last year, and the ewes already up the mountain, isn't it? And what about the wedding? How do they think he can be getting married if he is living up at the hafod? What excuse did he need?

But you love to see him holding up a flat stone like hymns in one hand, deciding where it shall go. Like a lawgiver, frowning, and whistling that tarantara rhythm with his teeth at his lower lip. 'Where . . . ta, ta, ta, ta . . . shall it . . . go . . . ta, ta . . .'

Tell Solon, the present is a stone that has no history when you look at it.

The barren sheep are already on the mountain and the sheep who lost their lambs. You walk up there into their exile, through Llain and Cae rwyn, up the hill, striking for the mountain path above the rock that always echoes 'No' whatever you shout. Do you think you might be welcome there in that rocky parlour where they chew and the thyme creeps down from clefts? Do you wish you were of their sterile kind, unperturbed, too idle to be startled, their blurred eyes like the stripes of bees?

No. No. No. No. No.

Tell Thales, nobody says 'Too late' if they can say nothing.

Thursday 28 May

Here it is, then, the symbol of the wedding to come, but if it is symbols you are thinking, is it not strange that the man provides the ring and the woman provides the finger?

The ring is to be placed on the finger that points least well.

The gold is changeless, the shape is without beginning, which again as symbols go is a lie to the individual life.

Tell Chilo, the 'O' of wonder is the echo of an echo.

Friday 29 May

You fear it, though you are allowed to show it as a seal of everything you needed to dispel fear. After showing, it is to be shut in its black box like a sleeping eye. God's knowing wink, says the devil in your belly. You say you love it.

In truth you prefer the puzzle ring he gave you at Christmas because it reminds you of what you know. This one is too solemn. It has secrets.

Tell Pittacos, we put on the future like the mask of our own face.

Saturday 30 May

Now all is a long excitement with the wedding four weeks off and your father making small beer. You wonder why he bothers to get out the cart and spend half an hour harnessing it just to go for Saturday tea to Ty-bach, but then he and Taid load it up with the beer tub on its heavy frame and on the way home you sit squeezed up at the front, with Twm perched on Buddug, driving the flies off with a handkerchief on a stick.

And it wants cleaning, doesn't it, with traces of yeast from Christmas mouldy and misbehaving? Twm says the malt is mouldy, too, and your father gives him a clip round the ear. He got the malt from Evan Williams, although your mother looks at him sharply, wondering what has been promised in return.

For hours on end you can forget. You feel protected now by all these arrangements.

But it does not forget you, even though it has nothing

to remember. Behind the auricular hillocks is the sound-lessness of everything still unheard. It needs no exhortation to action. The battle is all around, the girding, the darkness. Foot plates and ankles. Taking a stand.

Sunday 31 May

When you come back from Saron and he comes with you, you feel more than ever that you are both simply continuing something begun long before. In the shadow of your mother and father you seem to be seeing something through. What would he say about that? You would never be able to put it into words, and if you could, how could you not make it seem as though he were merely a bystander, a catalyst within the maternal family? It is your obligation to keep it up, his to assist you to do so. Which is why men are so irritating.

As now, with your father boiling up his gallons and getting in the way. And your mother moulding the apron to her palms:

'Do you have to do it on the Sabbath? You might have got it all done yesterday.'

You smile at Gruffudd. This intimacy in front of him, this contrived piety, this slight dignity in the preparations, this acceptance of him as someone not to be offended, this licence to fuss: you don't know if you are proud or critical of it.

You do not see that the tone is one that you, too, often

wear with him when he cannot or will not share your sense of what must be done.

Monday 1 June

At last the primitive heart divides. It is only one part of a continuous transformation, but it is nonetheless a hidden enchantment. And your own heart goes out mysteriously to Twm, as though ten years had rolled back and he were once again that expected surprise, that smell, that superfluity, that rival, that wrinkled doll. And you younger than he is now, as ready then to take guarded responsibility as he is now to wander off doing nothing at all.

You'd think Twm would be uncomfortable in his body, as though Nature were finding it hard to make anything of him at all, neither baby nor man, all limbs and restlessness.

But perhaps at this moment between transformations he is as much himself as he ever has been or ever will be. Do you ever miss being your real self?

Tuesday 2 June

Twm is forever peeping under the blanket to watch the drifting somersaults of the yeast.

He brings a stone from the stream he is damming to ask you if it is valuable.

He collects firewood for next winter, rotted fence-stumps and gorse boughs.

He breathes soap planets of trembling air.

He is everywhere and nowhere, under your feet and gone when you want him. He is a changeling, a spirit conjuring the elements.

Wednesday 3 June

There are fine things in your mother's wooden chest and they are now all yours for the saying. Practical things, and practical things made memorable with beautiful flourishes, like rooms in which music is played: runners with lace borders, caps with double laces, undergarments with stitching never to be seen. Such delicacy! You have often peeped in the chest, but never seen its treasures unfolded and laid out. Some handkerchiefs are like wisps of smoke, or like the shadows of butterflies that have momentarily rested against the clothes-line. And there is sound linen, stiff with yellowing folds, in crumpled paper smelling of violets.

There are things here that your mother was shown by her own mother, things perhaps that even your grandmother was so shown. How can life change when it is hoarded against change? It is worn away so slowly: slow as the wearing of unworn threads, slow as the stream stroking Twm's goblin doorstep of red serpentine, slow as dust-motes to settle in the shafts of June sun falling through the skylight on to the bed in which you were made. Its changes are only subtle variations on a familiar theme, like the bells of the town church when the ringers dip their knees. No wonder it is hardly noticed.

Thursday 4 June

Your father is trapping the genie of happiness in casks to be broached when such service is required. The tub tilts to let the amber stream flow out through its gorse filter.

The row of stout wooden stomachs standing there, unmoving and proud, promises much sound and movement. What can be going on invisibly inside them, the yeasts and sugars drizzling upwards in dizziness and air? The hatches are battened, the pirate cargo tethered and still, its journey simply a journey in time.

What does it remind you of?

Friday 5 June

Already the nostrils, lips, tongue, and the arms bent at the elbows. That alone would be determination enough to snuff up the world, enough to make a spoor of destiny.

To begin with it will be the nearest thing; finally it will be the farthest. The breast will be surrendered for language and that searching light in the eye will reflect horizons.

One day you will have to let it go.

Saturday 6 June

Causes have effects, but do all effects have causes? It's a matter of whether it's intention or recrimination. If you want something to happen it may very well do so if you help to bring it about, but you can sometimes ask 'why' till the cows come home.

Then when the cows do come home there is too much to be doing with them to bother.

Polly Parry used to say that kissing was the thing, and that once when she was taken to the dance at the assembly rooms in Caernarfon Captain Jenkyn tried to put seedcake in her mouth when he kissed her. Then they would have had to be married. She also said that babies were born out of the navel.

Did you ever believe anything that Polly said? One St John's Eve you caught snails together and looked at their tracks in the morning. She swore it was a dithering 'J', but you said it looked more like a vagrant 'S'. That and a dozen other prognostications were thoroughly forgotten when she married Jones y Felin, and became permanently grave.

What about your snail? Did it set out, remember something and then turn back in a roundabout sort of way?

Snails and babies bring their houses with them, but where are you going to live?

Sunday 7 June

The answer is: in Nant-y-cwm. It seems to be one of those decisions that no one ever quite remembers deciding, because speculation immediately revealed it as obvious. Nant-y-cwm, not half a mile from anywhere else. Nant-y-cwm, with two chimneys and twenty acres.

But where will little Edwin go, who has been keeping it aired ever since Mr Price's aunt died? If a man has planted barley, has he not a right to reap it?

Today is the calling of the banns, the 'too late' moment when all the unheard voices lay their claims: little Edwin and little Edwin's barley, the beautiful boy by the hawthorn hedge, and not least the still-drowned labials of the mer-miracle, drifting down there in its human fathoms with its webbed fingers and its stubby tail.

Monday 8 June

Little Edwin can be put up at Hendre-nant, if he can be put up with at all. He travels light, but lies heavy. He owns nothing, but once he has sat down you can hardly get him up again.

Power is all excuses, and privilege a ritual of bargaining. They will hear more of little Edwin's jokes and smell more of his farts. He can be told to do more, or told more often to do something. The result might just be that he is actually more useful.

They will let him reap his barley.

Tuesday 9 June

This is another reason for you to be beholden to Mrs Price. You are beholden as much for what she retains as for what she gives up. Whatever she produces establishes her at the centre of its production, wherever it ends up. She has cast the threads to trace it back again, like the stitches on his shirts which her fingers have woven, tiny threaded traces like the steps of wagtails in the snow, marks of determination that hang at wrist, shoulder and throat, the gathering of girded robes, the facings and panels of the week's work, clean and mended.

His whole body is like this. It is in her care and in her gift.

Wednesday 10 June

Whatever you do with that body, it will never be yours as it has been hers. It can only be yours to the extent that it has become his own. A man may never come fully into the possession of his body. There will always be something about it that puzzles him, that doesn't quite know what it is for. Let it perform to cheers, twice-nightly to a full house. Let it be unrivalled in strength, and in endurance. Let it sleep the utterly satisfied sleep of the beast. Still, somewhere, somehow, there is that little unsettling corner of doubt. The dust behind the door. A place unreached by the brisk broom of understanding. A place of darkness, and mysterious noises.

And he doesn't know if the mystery is about origins or about destinations. For he is lost between them.

Thursday 11 June

For you, though, because it is all mystery it is all peace. You have at last been bequeathed to yourself. Your body is running beside you, like a crowd. It is a ritual procession. It is adoration.

Given and received in ignorance, it lives in you like pure knowledge.

Friday 12 June

And what will therefore happen when it is fully known? For every action there must be a counter-action. For every involuntary event, a corresponding frustration. How can you undo something that you have not consciously done?

The great bed that is carried in pieces in the cart to Nant-y-cwm, carved like tablets of the Law, seems like part of the puzzle. Three pieces, three bloodless moons. One, two, three.

It is as though if he could put it together differently it might turn out not to be a bed at all, but the prow of a sailing vessel with the direction as surely lodged within it as it is in a compass. Or part of a scaffold; hanged at the yard-arm; a trap.

Such is the nature of this adventure, after all. But the Law is only roses and lilies, and Buddug goes at a friendly trot.

Saturday 13 June

Departure for the Islands of the Blessed. Those who sail there are too contented to report back, or too ashamed. The distance travelled was formerly space, unilluminated and directionless. It is becoming a route for broken messages from the supernatural tour-guide. Make of them what you will. They are hardly better understood by you than by all the others. Already you are waving to the shore. Already the little stowaway is perfectly safe. The webs are breaking, the fingers and toes preparing to curl. The ankles might grow wings, hovering above like one of the twelve kindly little winds. So what, then, of it? And him?

Could he actually see it, he would acknowledge it now as of his kind, no longer a hunch-headed shrimp, no longer a spade-handed squirt, a tailed bubble-boulder, a knotted trail of snot, an outrageous festering spot. Could he see the little bugger now, he might take off altogether.

If nobody knows, he knows least of anybody, since it is he who should suspect. He is waving too, now.

The shore recedes.

Sunday 14 June

What of the planet of love? The island where it is born is all boundary, more and more differentiated, like a granite coast, shape and liquid of the opening shell, serration of the shore. Gender is a good question. The definition is specific but not obvious. If it is female, it will perpetuate the mystery, the nested matrices, the sloughing of gratified pods. If it is male, Gruffudd will feel flattered. He will have a foot in the door, a spy in the camp. Let him therefore be ignorant. It will not be spoken of again.

Monday 15 June

His business is elsewhere, on the rigging, in the crow's nest, at the guns. His flags run up passwords to establish the identity of friends. He steers broadside to threaten foes.

What is privately a puzzle is publicly a joke. All that comes to pieces will be found to fit perfectly. And the men respond mutinously, in laughter, in drinks. Dandi Pugh says, with a friendly arm on the shoulder:

'Have you filled her sail with wind yet, Gruffudd? Have you feathered your nest? Have you jumped the gun? Are you sailing for a storm?'

Have others solved the puzzle before him? He clearly has some catching up to do.

Tuesday 16 June

There is always one planet you can't sail by, and that is the planet you sail on. There is always a day beyond record or prediction, and that is today. There is always a destination for which there was no need to set out, and that is home.

Why on earth should Gruffudd be ill at ease? Is it that his planet has shifted? Did he want no adventures at all?

Wednesday 17 June

His future changes shape so quickly, like the function of the puzzle shapes. Take them to pieces and put them together again, and what do you have? Where you had last breath, now you have first breath. Where you had blessings, now you have blushing. Even the roses and lilies have a meaning that they didn't have.

No use thinking that beds are for sleeping. Beds are for bobbing. Beds are for babies.

Thursday 18 June

Above all there is the understanding presence of the father of the gods. Severe, remote, but amused at these little difficulties. Master of horoscopes, he knows everything to come. He is historian of the forgotten and the fatuous, scientist of the accidental, inquisitor of intentions.

Tune to his moods and nothing will come right. If you go after a lost lamb, you lose its brother. If you piss on the pass, the wind changes direction. If you grin ruefully when you hit your thumb with a hammer, you'll hit it twice. If you think the sermon may be referring to you, you're right.

If you woo the tallest girl on the mountain, she'll lead you by the nose.

Friday 19 June

And then there is the absence of the most remote, the furthest orbit within which complete lives are shaken and rolled and come to rest. Here the singing of the blessed is loudest, but it is on the other side of a door that he can never expect to be opened.

He only knows it as the door closed on the granting of wishes, the rattling knob of wagers, the keyhole of trusting to chance. He could live his whole life leaning slumped against it, his elbows on his knees and his wrists turned out. Like the gypsy boy with the dog outside the public bar at Ty-goch, listening to the beer loosening men's belts and tongues but hearing no secrets, the boy you saw across the hedge.

'Oh and the wonder of it! She with such a tongue, and he'll never say a word. And both of them together as thick as bread.'

Saturday 20 June

The hayfield is to be finished today. Your father said it was too early, but Taid's big toe had been telling him of rain at the end of the month, and next week would be busy with the wedding. Your mother said so, and not much she ever said was wrong.

The new moons travel into the standing grasses, which sigh together and lean in swatches. You and your mother and your Aunt Ann, Hefyd Hughes and her sister Sally, little Edwin and mad William from Cwm. The burnished blades sever and gather in one motion, the timing of the strokes almost together and in order, like bells.

Twm is master of the sharpening stone, which he has oiled till it lies as dark and heavy in his hand as Ynys Fawr in high spray. Your father and Taid, and Gruffudd for the first time this year, tie the hay into stooks.

The hayfield gets smaller as it is cut. Not only the dwindling patch of standing grasses, but the shape of the field itself. And you think, appropriately, that size is only a function of what constitutes it. When will it show? Perhaps not for a very long and precariously safe time. And just as you think this, straightening yourself, and wiping the sweat from your forehead with the back of your hand, another rabbit bolts naked from the populated sanctuary of the grass.

Sunday 21 June

It will itself bolt when its time comes, but not in defeat. It will take its chance at the propitious moment, like an emperor surveying a battlefield. Already, in a manner of speaking, it seems to do so. It is the considered squint of envisaged victory, though there is nothing yet to be seen.

Now the stubble has expanded to its three hedges and the path by the west wall where couples walked with casual connivance, in hope of a hiding, awr ar y gwair. These June days are almost over, and as ever, an hour in the hay has itself expanded to a lifetime out of it. This is the sermon of the grass.

Monday 22 June

Now the year is almost suspended. If you go down to the wood you will hear the fair folk at their polkas.

Keep your distance, or they will be more than usually

44

interested in you. They are nosy for news and hungry for humans. They will nudge you and tickle you, and blow into your nostrils as gypsies calm horses. They are so small that they can dazzle you by skating on your eyeball like a pond. Their orchestras whine in your ear and you scratch in places where they have been dancing.

They will know your secret in an instant, and they will want it for themselves. They will shout with delight, and soundlessly the moon will sail out from behind the clouds. The twisted silvery branches of the oaks will draw you deeper into the wood where the troops of fair folk give you their whole attention.

They scale you down and shiver your nape. They mumble your moles and dampen your snatch. Every cable of your hair is lifted free for your head to sail on its startled voyage, and the body follows as if in a dream, the nipples as saddles to lead the procession.

You are their cow in calf brought home for its cream. They stroke your fullness and tremble your flanks. You are their prize and the night is your pasture. Beware!

Tuesday 23 June

It is Midsummer Eve, and time now hangs between the path of the sickle and the tying of the sheaf. You are yours and not yours. You are his and not his. You are lost, even your nose is lost, to your parents.

You could fly away now, for in the space between

events nothing can happen and anything you do will be imaginary and miraculous.

Grip the grey fur with your knees (is it a mouse or is it a moth?) and use your apron as reins. There is a whirring and a clatter and you are in the air, half-choked with pollen. The red eyes glow like lamps in front of you, lighting a path through the night.

Wednesday 24 June

Everything seems to have been arranged without you taking heed. You have been in your dreams for weeks, dreams like the seething of the ale, dreams like the fluttering of the linen, dreams of an old house that will be your new house, dreams of fairies.

Your mother catches you motionless, staring at nothing, and she laughs: 'You great thing.'

Not for you the definitions of guests and the boundaries of meat and cheese, the inclusion of hymns and the exclusion of jellies, the limits of fiddling and decisions about forks and jugs.

As well a bed had sheets and a pump be well oiled, as well a dairy possessed a churn and a cupboard be stocked with candles.

And Megan undertaking the cake, and Mr Unwin for buttonholes, and Dandi Pugh for the bidding.

It all passes you by, like everything in your life that ever was, like the slops of the sea.

Thursday 25 June

The day is near, but somehow he is not near. Does he feel he must keep his distance? Once he brought you gifts, frequent enough to make you not forget, rare enough to surprise; small things sometimes, lavender, a pullet's egg in a nest of moss and stonecrop; or treasures, the puzzle ring, the spoon he carved with the chain intact as if to make sugar a prison. Sometimes they were left on the step and it was known what they were and who they were for, and even Twm wouldn't dare to touch the straw doll or the crimson apple. A fairy would have been well pleased with such offerings, and they seemed to give you a fairy's grace. You came and went with contentment, lighter of foot, thoughtful as if considering favours.

Friday 26 June

The joke is perfectly true: there is still time to change your mind. You guess that he is hearing the joke more than you are, going along with it, even making it himself, grinning into his drink. Still time to change your mind, but not to change your body.

That crow passing by thinks it howlingly funny. As it passes into the ash tree by the stream it is almost slapping its thighs with laughter.

The crow draws a tankard of ale and sets it down in front of Gruffudd. For a moment it stands by, arms

47

akimbo, like a waiter at the Undertaker's Ball. It raises its eyebrows. Will he drink or won't he?

Gruffudd puts out his hand uncertainly, not sure which tankard to take.

The crow is off again. Its cackle turns to a grumble, and it disappears down the valley.

Saturday 27 June

Everyone seems to be running. Nothing stays still enough to be recognised. Nothing is ever quite its own shape.

Things were clearer when you married llwy and fforch in a ceremony under the kitchen table, with an egg cosy hat and a sermon from the salt box. There was time enough then, for a spoon and a fork know well enough what they have to do with each other, and will do nothing else.

And Nain took the spoon, and showed you, with her two knuckles and her moving thumb, the little reflection in it of the fat lady scrubbing her back in the bath.

Running downstairs, running upstairs, running with flowers. And you dressed in clothes you never saw your mother wear. The stream running blind as ever it did and Twm running to dress Buddug in ribbons. And running up the village street Hughes aunts and Price cousins and Mr Unwin distributing roses.

In the eye of the storm, the resolute profile of Gruffudd

staring out a hymn, his moustache severely trimmed and a cut on his jaw. And the words to be said as they have been said for weeks in your head and are now said for the last time, the ring is put on, and suddenly all the men are really running.

They are running as if the altar is ablaze, as if there were a pot of gold over the crest of the hill. Eyes fixed, chests puffed tight in waistcoats, hats in their hands, knees and elbows going like pistons, the crows mocking them from the graveyard trees. Their shapes are nothing but the shape of laughter.

Only Gruffudd does not run, having no need of the bride cake since he has won the bride.

Llwy kissed fforch, and fforch bowing stiffly kissed llwy, and then there would only be the two bare knuckles and the lifelike movement in the little scratched metal mirror, the mystery of the momentary body, the vision of the naked fat lady who will never turn round.

Sunday 28 June

As there is a sun and a moon in the heavens, and a king and queen on their thrones, and as the hearth is divided between kettle and tobacco, so there shall be man and woman. Your father and mother have proved it, and the preacher said so clearly when he sermonised from the Book of Begetting, two by two, and all the generations, and Adam in the lonely garden.

But nobody said anything about Eve in the garden. She might have raised Cain all by herself and been called holy for it.

Is that what they mean by 'my cup runneth over'? You feel him against you, more like two bodies than one, and it is the same as the parlour floor again, only lawful, and there is less cotton between you.

And there is no laughing and talking, for it is a mystery and the cup runneth over and there is sighing and holding.

Monday 29 June

'On the third day he rose again' are the words that come straight into your head. And somewhere behind them, too, is something said by Dandi Pugh in a way that you would prefer to forget, something he could not have dared to say out of his character as gwahoddwr, which he still held himself to possess when he called to inform you that the sum entered into his account book for the bidding was £14 8s. 6d. and that the money was already in Gruffudd's hands.

'I hope your young husband is an upright man.'

It is like dreams, to be dismissed from your waking life, or visions and their deep reflections, the angel of the hawthorn hedge who stirred the unsuspecting pool of your still life once and to this day, i lencyn ar ei drafel, the young man on his travels. In the ordinary traffic of the house not a word to be breathed, but at night now, an expectation.

You would not be Moley Mair, the tall terror you once were, if you were not impulsively curious. You are bound to lift his night-shirt to view this monument, for you have paid more than your ha'penny to climb to the top.

Look, look, you can see over Penllechog to Gurn Ddu!

But not for long. This monument doesn't care to be looked at, for all it has accomplished in the darkness. It lowers you down, gently, like the head of the kneeling elephant when the Maharajah descends. Nor does it care to be referred to, unlike (to take the only comparable example) Twm's jimmy, which is a pale little shrimp of a thing, with a sprung bounce to it, and a slight kink, and an utter obliviousness to any future responsibilities that might be hanging over it.

Oh, this one feels its responsibilities all right, and guards them guiltily in deep folds and wrinkles, like a snake that slithers out of sight into the roots of the heather.

Tuesday 30 June

Your finger, his ring. A russula in moss, the dome hidden, feeling for its rim. His finger, your ring. But he doesn't find it.

Each night there is something different to do, a different place for the spill, a different moment for the sigh. But the spider on the beam hasn't moved, its head cradled in its legs, a picture of melancholy and caution. Sometimes, like tonight, you feel like a spider yourself at the centre of your circular world, wishing webs.

Or like a fish, for whom conception is external and completed. Mr Fish squirts and is gone. He is soon breathing deeply.

All this is a sort of charade, you realise, for it is far too late to stage a valid conception. How soon will it be before he knows?

Wednesday 1 July

Soon enough, as it happens. The day might have been merely one in a series of unexceptional days, the first Wednesday of many such Wednesdays in a married life. You take three herrings that you had from Megan in exchange for a pound of butter. Their size and weight in your hand unnerves for a moment the knife that opens their bellies. You are an avenging fury, a Judith.

The twin roes are snug as kernels and the colour of batter, but netted at the tips with the veins that tether them, like bloodshot eyes. Hardly a tug and they slip over your watery fingers. They won't stay still on the plate.

He is tired from helping little Edwin to harvest his barley, which means that it was little Edwin who helped him. He eats two herrings, and all the roes, and drinks a bottle of the small beer left over from the bidding.

The result is that within a minute of blowing out the candle he is inside you for the first time, being in no state to stage the rude act to his conscious satisfaction and therefore without much anxiety. The anxiety is all yours, and it undoes you.

'Oh, you mustn't harm him!'

Your choice of pronoun is instinctive. There is another that might have gone unnoticed.

Thursday 2 July

Moley Mair, this moment had to come! It is like a door at long last opened suddenly closed again.

Does he think it an impostor or a fantasy? Just for a moment you felt him react with a leap of unnatural logic, that of course weddings make babies. This morning there is still that stubborn wish in his soft brown eyes to resort to such an immediate explanation of consequence, but really it is all up with you now. The little lodger has been writing the story of its own shape for eleven weeks now, and though you can't feel it yet, it is starting to move. There is no mistaking it. The top-heavy fish-lump, all spine and folds, is now day by day more recognisably human. The face, from being a goggling reptilian slit with nasal pits like the twin adits of a mine, is now something you might smile at on a sunny morning.

But Gruffudd is not smiling.

He has for the moment no relationship with it at all except one of disbelief. It is more invisible than the paddling mole, and leaves fewer signs. It is tinier than the lark and does not sing. It is less comprehensible than the ostrich of New South Wales, for it has been seen by no one.

He can understand little Edwin's toothache because he has had one himself, though he can't feel Edwin's.

If it is true, it is like living his life backwards.

A man imagining his rivals is the most abject creature in the whole world. Did you once tell him of your Cousin Owen? Very well, then. Today he will even be humiliated by Cousin Owen, though Cousin Owen has been dead for over three years, found in a bog face down and peppered with his own lead. You dressed his knee as a child, and borrowed a kiss which he paid back in a different place.

That place is unrecoverable as Vortigern's grave, though Gruffudd might walk in his wondering for ever and ever in the lovely Nant Gwtheyrn of your neck and shoulders. But kisses are like the leaves of the tree. They are forgotten, and they come again, and they are much the same. If you keep still, they will grow.

54

Sunday 5 July

Today being Sunday he must have holy thoughts, and take you to chapel where you shall both appear to be happy. But there the first man he lays eyes on is mad William from Cwm, who once showed him something foul in a tin. Do you often take the leafy path through Cwm, where the bull stares out through a wooden chink, knee-deep in its own filth? And might not mad William have shown you his tin, too, and perhaps worse, having no idea of distinctions, and propriety, and respect? Mad William in his straddled posture, his pointing, and his caked trousers? What might that have led to, in your curiosity and shame?

Gruffudd knows that you go where you choose to, without hesitation.

Monday 6 July

He knows nothing of mealy Maelon who was moved to oratory when you bent over to haul the sack he brought and your taut haunches were like the Pillars of Hercules, a vision of the unexplored universe to a Phoenician trader. He put his hand there, gentle as stroking a cat, and gave you a cartwheel tuppence to complete the transference. The flour was not bedded in its sacking with greater compliance than your tilted hip supporting your elbow as you turned the heavy copper with your finger. For his own fingers had made your whole body from nape to knees feel like that sunk silky powder. A sluicing of milk might have made a batter of you. You could think of no rebuttal to his compliment, though you had no wish to pay him in his own coin.

Gruffudd is ready to think of a thousand such feelings.

Tuesday 7 July

He is perfectly ready to loathe all males for being males, particularly any he has reason to believe are long, confident and ready. If fruit were steel, magnetised at the poles. If a tree had the muzzle of a puma. If insolence should be admired. Then the world he was born into was truly a place of seething hypocrisy, where the battles that secretly raged were not about ideas or ideals but display and potency, the butt and thrust from a place of vantage, the slung heavy seed, the strut, the velvety antler. And the defeat of innocence.

In the small hours he is frozen in self-abasement at your searching hand, with the worst images he can muster. Your greed for any and everybody, even Iolo the Basket, who has never grown out of defying disbelief in the playground and was once known to have taken to going up the hill to call softly at your window though you were no more than a child. And, in a spirit of demonstration and challenge, watered your gate.

Wednesday 8 July

Were you not rumoured to have spoken with Mr Driscoll? That distant personage resplendent in brown and yellow surfaces, leather and wool, with all the necessary laces and buckles, and an abundance of hair and cravat? Aloft and staring down from his horse, all thigh, boot and stirrup?

What might have come of that? Did anything come of it? Is it known what he said?

Something looked into you from his eyes which made you remember them, and anyone who loves you, looking into your eyes, might see it too, and feel haunted. Blank and alive, like a dull responsible puddle of quicksilver.

Did you receive it like a message from an irresponsible god, an arrow with feathers at its heels?

Thursday 9 July

He eats your meals, but he has gone silent. Is he now thinking of Dafydd Thomas? From his point of view this is the individual of whom he might most reasonably be jealous, since Dafydd attended you closely for a whole season, giving everyone the opportunity to notice that he was quite as tall as you. And since Dafydd is tall in spirit, too, he is the greater threat, as being too circumspect to marry a girl so compliant, if compliant you were. It is all perfectly clear to his tortured imagination, except that you are forced to point out that you have not walked

57

with Dafydd Thomas since last September, when, with your apron full of green hazelnuts, you told him that it was all up between you because you now knew that Gruffudd Price was the man for you.

How sad, for he was nothing but himself, after all, and could train a dog better than anyone, and gave you a sixpence with Queen Anne's face on it that looked like Mrs Parry sitting by the fire. And not one of the hazelnuts contained anything but damp air, they having been brought down early by an unseasonal wind.

Friday 10 July

When, at the end of this week of wondering, you at last challenge his obtuseness he has nothing left to hurt himself with except his own pride. For you point out that when he came into your skirts on the parlour floor he was closer to you than any man had ever been (and quite as close as men sometimes get, you might add, from your subsequent experience, though you keep your silence on that point, out of hope and charity). And then he weeps a little at the sense of missing something of himself in his own life, and at his own folly, and at his failure to match his dream of you with the present reality.

There is a stone in his soul which is like the shadow of the child, and it will not be shifted until he can be the father of the child in understanding as well as in deed (and in the fullness of the deed as well as in his understanding).

This is a trick which may be hard to perform. There is a demon on his shoulders inhibiting the careless ease of movement and gesture needed to bring it off. This demon announces that he is after all going to join his cousins at the hafod. The demon needs solitude. The demon needs to spite you, and to challenge you to love him.

The demon has no idea that in your heart you are half-wondering what it might have been like to love the gypsy boy with the golden hair who sang you such a prophetic song across the hawthorn hedge. For it is in the nature of love to feed on adventure as well as on trust. Thwarted in one it will turn to the other.

Saturday 11 July

Love lets on long leases and allows excuses. What is weeping at night is reasons by day, and the parties to the bond connive at the substitution. What hasn't long been held can lightly be let go. The lighter, the stronger, like wool tightly spun. And the reasons are for the inquisitive world to turn over, which it will, and worse, if they are not held with pride and a toss of the head that says that is the way you want it. For the moment it will have to be the way it suits you. And me.

But his weakness has to become your strength, and so

your excuses by day are also weeping at night, for tears must never show. And like the wool drawn out by the spinning mule the distance he travels from you will have to be the distance he will eventually return, for you have held his body once and for all; you have made him the father he is in act and fact, which now are one, as the strands twine.

Sunday 12 July

Like body, like ghost. In his anger he wants to leave nothing with you at all. He wants to waste all tenderness, like fruit from a fruiting tree, and to shake it till the branches are bare. There is no small thought or sentiment he will not kill.

He kills it because he wants you to bring it to life. He wants to be rescued from his own misery, which is his failure to know what he should be doing and how he should do it. He would rather the fruit rot. He does not begin to think that the tree might not bear again. The tree is yours, and he fears you like a sibyl with secrets, as though your magic with rowan and elder were to charm him into a circle where he would lose all movement.

Ghost draws him there. He came at a call and stood foolishly for a moment within the circle, hearing the truth and terrified by it. Now he is going. The prince breaks his sword on a stone and conjures spooks to send him howling.

To make him stay at least for chapel, to be seen together and seem to share his strange plan, costs you a cut finger as you savagely saw the bread down like his neck, a stroke for each righteous tearful word.

Well, he will go tomorrow, then.

Monday 13 July

Ghost goes and body goes, but leaves a hostage which the world will soon know of. Heavens, that's such an old story, let the world make of it what it will.

We have no need of him. He has been plucked. Let him dry in the rafters. There is a time and a season for everything.

We have much to talk about, you and I. Soon you will begin to talk to me as I talk to you. Meanwhile you will forgive my sermonising.

Tuesday 14 July

In the beginning everything was weighed against itself and the scales went neither up nor down.

Do not believe what you are told in Saron about Chaos the primal mother and Word the male command. For the void contains all idea of form, and the darkness all creation.

It is the darkness that makes weight, and gravity that makes gravid. Today is the day that your mother must know it, who has known it before for herself.

It makes her sit down as if she hadn't seen that the chair was there, and did not care. Her contemplation of the fact is as theoretical as the whole of posterity. She sees it as copperplate on a Bible leaf, not as the little rapscallion it already is, leaking like an old man into its sac and blithely drinking its own piss as though the planet would spin for ever in astonishment.

Wednesday 15 July

And the spirit of restlessness and dissatisfaction said: 'Let there be light!' And the light was as the light of reason and the questioning of the darkness.

And day and night were divided, bringing sorrow. For what was accomplished in darkness was undone in the light, and the questioning made light of the darkness and reduced it to a rule.

Thursday 16 July

And her mother and her mother's mother knew it, for the history of Europe is the history of twenty-seven generations, and the history of the living world is as proportionately little. Every womb was created in a womb just like itself, matter enfolded in matter to the beginning.

And the spirit of restlessness and dissatisfaction looked upon the teeming waters and made division of them, and reduced them to scale. The vault of the heavens breeding gases, and the dense stars. And the one was set to watch the other.

Solid is an illusion, a trick manifestation of the invisible. Its forms are a parody of our notion of the idea, which the rational light has beamed upon like a smug father. Poor father! He can invent a cup, a cupboard or a church, since his head is a similar container and his busy mind goes about attempting to perfect its idea. This idea is simply to ask questions of all that resists questioning. Turn the cup upside down and the wine will spill. Why? Open the cupboard and put the bread inside. Close it and make the bread disappear. How? Enter the church and claim that you yourself have disappeared. When?

The answers are written in dry dust under a hot sun.

And the waters were not gathered, but instead were divided into seven seas, which is nothing but the number by which the light tries to make sense of itself. And the first symbol of the life enclosed by its masters was the Mediterranean, which celebrated rule and scale, and the myth of the waiting woman.

Sunday 19 July

And the second symbol was the Baltic, from which the masters fled, fearing to be lured into its deeps. The terrified tribes brought with them a new myth, of the fatal woman.

Monday 20 July

From the Arctic, where lights stained the air like radiant hair and the gnawed bone rocked on the threshold, came the myth of the devouring woman.

Tuesday 21 July

From the Antarctic, where straight lines are uncertain and the only regularity is darkness, came the myth of the invisible woman.

64

Wednesday 22 July

A sea which is a true sea will come up to its coasts like an inquisitive animal, lured by the fragrance and by the weeping: from the Indian Ocean came the myth of the captive woman.

Thursday 23 July

Where the wind blows strongest there will be voyages, and where there are voyages there will be partings: from the Atlantic came the myth of the unfaithful woman.

Friday 24 July

And then when the clouds roll back and the sky is a perfect shell, when the line is fulfilled in the circle, and horizon confirms that the only land is now contained by sea, the light and the life negotiate in the Pacific the myth of the desirable woman.

Saturday 25 July

So for a man the woman is a home that will always be there, the place he has come from and will eventually go to. For him, the interim is exile. The story of his life is the adventure of categories, the licensing of names, the geography of his exile.

Sunday 26 July

And the spirit of restlessness and dissatisfaction saw the life and feared it for the seed within it which was sufficient and grew in darkness, herb, wort, weed, root and tuber. And the struggle towards the light was called death.

Monday 27 July

And when the root became a mouth this was a signal for movement and for universal death, as the creatures came out of the dark waters to seek the light, to walk the world and to fall from the air.

Aiguillette, quivering in the marsh. Button-sized birds, never at rest. Cormorant, who conducted the wind. Digger rats. Elephantasy, extruding folds. Fastitocalon, on whose weedy back sailors lit a fire and danced. Goldfinch, flattened against the side of a tree. Horse, the philosopher. Ice-beetles. Jelly-whiskers. Kraken, barely breathing. Lord Slaver. Millilegged bad-boys clustering in rot. Narwhal, colour of a corpse. Otter, lither than water. Pleasure-seeking heron. Quickhatch, soon fledged. Rock-skinned softies. Salad snails. Tiger, walking in his breath. Urdu-speaking baboons. Viper, pleased with his pattern. Worms a day away from their tails. Xylophagous beetles. Yak, humped and grunting. Zebra, photographing shadows.

Tuesday 28 July

And the earth shook with the tread of the dying.

Wednesday 29 July

And the first idea of the spirit of restlessness and dissatisfaction was to explain death by devouring its products, hunting and gathering, pasture and vintage, breeding and slaughter.

Thursday 30 July

And the second idea was the creation of God in its own image, which was the image of man and his dissatisfactions. It was the image of regulation, and the image of fear, and he had dominion over the dying.

Friday 31 July

And on the seventh day there was no rest, for the spirit was restless, and this day was not the day of rest but the day of sacrifice, when the spirit created the female and went to her in shame and loneliness and bound her in servitude.

Here endeth the lesson.

Saturday 1 August

But you have nothing to say to me yet, have you? That will come. That will come when you not only know that you are a mother, but know that you are a mother before you are a daughter.

You are between worlds now. You have left your family before you have one. You have left a mother before you are one. You have left a father and have lost another. You have ceased to be a child before you have had one. But all this will be reconciled.

Think: this is the fulfilment of the body and of its purest pleasure, the pleasure in itself. Your mother puts her hand to your cheek and cradles your chin. She recognises this assumption of yourself. It is like the calm of your first sleep, a glimpse of pure being that found echoes in many childhood moods but was never fulfilled till now. For a moment your jaw moves as if you were going to speak. Its muscle tenses against her fingers. You look quickly at her and away, wiping your hands.

She looks at you with nothing more to say. With everything to say.

Sunday 2 August

Saron, Saron, why must you go on about pain? It was not my doing. It is a man's fear, a man's guilt, which he hides in bristly eyebrows. The preacher has bristly eyebrows that tend to make vertical lines above his eyes, like a demon. And it was the demon who spoke: 'In sorrow thou shalt bring forth children.'

When the preacher is not being a preacher he is walking with his dog. You'd think him quite harmless, but he is a Manichee. Even your mother will hear him but not listen, and it will take a week of celebrating the portals of the body to forget the admonitions of this Sunday.

Monday 3 August

Your mother will help you, that much now is certain. You remember, in a great flood that leaves you helpless on her shoulder, all her love for you in the days of your childhood. She takes your hand and weeps with you for the fingers it wore in your innocence. When you came in chapped from the mountain, building your own walls for the lambs you could never catch, she called you her bysedd cochion, and later when that flower grew dusty and tall she showed you what she meant by putting a foxglove bell on each of your own red fingers. The touch of her hands always conveyed purpose in its tenderness, putting on butter and pressing the moisture outwards from the back of the hand across the roughened pudge of the knuckles and down each finger in turn. Every finger had its share of attention, like a little batch to be kneaded.

How different from Gruffudd, who turned it over to look at the underside! Did he think you had palmed his soul, like a fortune-teller?

Tuesday 4 August

Earlier you can't remember, though you know you eagerly fastened your lips to the buds of that tree in whose branches you lay cradled. Sour as dough, sweet as sap, salt as earth, original of all taste. But a tree whose roots are forgotten, a tree that flowers perpetually, blossom blossoming with blossom, a little love curled in an intaglio of petals like a nude bee, printed by God for a foundling of Nature, a text to be storied ('Fy maban! O fy maban!') as a defiance of danger, a revelation of infinite providence, the baby smiling and showing no signs of fear. Little gift.

How long will it take to come into his arms and show no fear? To see no signs of it in him? The mouth is the busiest of the seven portals of the face.

Wednesday 5 August

Your mother has always smelt of growing things, the substances that grow and enable growth. On her apron the palm marks of bread in its dry infancy, the crushed grain of the wheat that blowing turns into a cloud, a white dispersal like souls in torment, waiting for the holy touch of water to congregate into a loaf. On her fingers the balm of herbs crushed and broken from their roots (which uncompromisingly shoot again) to give their savour to the pot: especially the uncut jewels of shallots, whose unparcelling provokes tears of their own shape; and mint, standing in the stream like a flag as if to celebrate the Sunday whose noon it fragrantly seasons.

Bubble, bubble, bubble. Potatoes thudding in the pan, and the steam of mint over all, like a tent.

Thursday 6 August

Why is the thudding so comforting? It is like the thunder that lulled you before your first uncurling, the undertow and beat of blood in the darkness. It is the seal of Sunday, the drum that heralds dinner, and your mother dragging across your mouth the damp flannel that reeks of cellars. And other sounds. The murmur of a voice and stories in your attic; and riddles:

> 'Beth sydd miwn a beth sydd mas,
> Dyw e ddim miwn na mas?'

You know the answer to that one, as you snuggle down into the bedclothes, your chin on the sheet like a bookmark. What is in and out, and is neither in nor out?

There is another darkness that steals in every day when the sun is not looking, and it rattles the window-catch and will not go away until you close your eyes. Will the window keep it out, as it keeps the light of your candle in? The window, that open surface that is neither in nor out?

Your window is like the house's eye. The curtain shuts it like an eyelid. Once in childish slumber, now like a terrible wink.

Friday 7 August

And opens it again on a new morning, and your mother already up and feeding the hens. If you shut your eyes she is not there, and if you open them again she hasn't ceased to be busy. She is still casting scraps with that guarded generosity of motion which casts flour on to the table before the dough is turned out or seed into the furrow when she walks behind your father guiding Buddug in the field that is destined for cabbages. But when your eye opens she is in a different position. Nothing stops when you don't see it.

And now Gruffudd being at the hafod is like a great closing of the eye of your marriage. A curtain has been tugged across not as a protection against the darkness but as a defiance of light, a shrinking, a bleakness, like being put to bed in the afternoon with a fever.

All the time he will be living his stupid torment. He is deaf to the silent words in your head, far from your fingers, far from the smell of your hair, the tilted sup of your lips, your receiving gaze. What is he up to, that coward? What have his thoughts brought him to? Nothing stops when you don't see it.

Saturday 8 August

One divided becomes two, but two divided is less than one, restless and incomplete. It is no good bringing arithmetic into biology for even your worse halves are uncertain fractions, and fractious halves only certain of their own incompletedness. No unity knows it is one, till sorrow makes for yearning. The split of mother and child is not the same as the split of wife and husband, for it comes into being in yearning, when the cord is cut. Any woman and any man may fadge without that severance, but now a kind of cord is cut between you and him.

You've only the mind now to try to work it out.

Sunday 9 August

Why do men and women marry at all? The demon Manichee would thump it out thus: it is a state that those who are in, desire to get out of, and those who are out, wish to enter. It is a blessing to a few, a curse to many, and a great uncertainty to all. If the spirit has a vocation, it should be pursued single-mindedly. The world has been peopled in weakness. But it is better to marry than to burn.

Today you sit in Saron with your mother and father and Twm, and you feel like goods returned to the manufacturer. As though this is where the recognisable parts of you really belong, two noses of a similar model, a set of lips; warp of colour, weft of will; miscellaneous items ticked off; unusual qualities, humour, voice, tallness. Serviceable in its way, just not what was ordered.

What did he once say? 'All women must get married; but no men.'

Dead-pan, the finger lightly drawn across beneath the moustache, lifting it slightly, as though to an angle appropriate for wit.

Monday 10 August

Fix him in your sights, as though seeing him for the first time. What is he doing? Is he turned towards you or away from you? Is he talking or is he silent? What is he wearing? Is he indoors or outdoors?

It doesn't matter. The attention is everything. You want to be alone, so that you can imagine him fully, and control that image in your head, but now that your secret is out you are as much visited as an oracle at the navel of the world.

The kettle is never off the boil.

Tuesday 11 August

It is Tuesday, and Polly Jones (Parry that was) has come to tell you of all the worst things that can befall the gravid mother. If there is anything terrible, she knows what it is, as for example Dandi Pugh's aunt was surprised by a mouse that ran out of a water jug when she went to the dresser. She dropped the jug into pieces and put her hand up to her cheek in fright. Now would you believe it, but when Dandi's little cousin was born he had a birthmark in just the very same place, and it was in the certain shape of a mouse?

You will take care, you tell Polly, not to touch any part of yourself in a moment of fear.

The absence of Gruffudd is remarked, but discussion avoided. The teapot is refilled.

Wednesday 12 August

Questions in order of frequency:

1. How do you know so soon? (This question disguised in a multitude of devious ways, the commonest by way of speculation upon the philosophy and emotions of Mr Hughes, who may be supposed, wrongly, to have put pressure on Gruffudd to do the right thing.)
2. How long have you known? (Corollary.)

3. Did he need persuading? (Allusions, in the most
    delicate manner, to the widely shared stories of little
    Edwin about your scenes with Gruffudd, seeking him
    out at all times of day to issue ultimatums.)
4. Did you need persuading? (A very different question,
    though ostensibly parallel.)
5. When is he coming back? (A question designed to
    elicit the answer to another, hidden question, i.e.
    'Why did he go?')

Some of these questions are not so far from your own.

Thursday 13 August

He might be even now standing as you are standing on
the doorstep, stretching slightly, rocking on his heels, a
cup of milk in your hands, warmed with a little honey.
Why not? You could lean against the door-frame as he
does, watching the morning light creeping by the trees in
the valley that still lie in mist. He could not help raising
his fingers to his hair at just the moment that you do the
same, stroking it back from the forehead.

   Might you meet in thought? You would like to think
so.

Friday 14 August

Each day at a different hour you have these precise
thoughts of him. You can barely visualise Uwch Hafotty,

though you have once seen it, a place of rough living, bunks and unplastered walls. It is enough to know him, and to know that he is living beyond the few poor days of wedded life you have had at Nant-y-cwm, in the negotiations of the roses and lilies, and trying as you are doing to take the measure of them.

How could you have told him, when you could hardly acknowledge that you knew yourself? When it made no sense at all to a rational creature? What was there to tell?

What, were you to believe after all in Polly's seedcake and Captain Jenkyn's foxy kiss?

This fluttering, so much a part of all that is expected, seems in itself unseasonal, like the butterfly in the window-pane, warmed by an April day and lured to its fatal early life. Could it not have waited and let the marriage catch up somehow? Like a lumbering quartet of slow iron-hooped wheels and its jolted startled passengers, following a bolted horse?

Saturday 15 August

In Nant-y-cwm, the stable door unbolted; in Uwch Hafotty, the horse's mouth closely examined.

In Nant-y-cwm, the quickening of the evidence; in Uwch Hafotty, the plaintiff turned judge.

In Nant-y-cwm, the defiance of death; in Uwch Hafotty, the denial of life.

77

In Nant-y-cwm, witness; in Uwch Hafotty, adjourn-
ment.

In Nant-y-cwm, two; in Uwch Hafotty, one.

Sunday 16 August

There is no possibility that can't for one gaunt moment
be entertained, no possibility either that isn't likely or
unlikely. There is no impossibility that should ever be
believed, nor any unlikelihood that is worth a moment's
consideration. And much that is likely can soon be proved
untrue. All this is unspeakable.

There is the loneliness of never having entered, and
there is the loneliness of having left.

There is the loneliness of exclusion, and the loneliness
of being simply in the wrong place.

All, too, unspeakable.

Monday 17 August

Poor Gruffudd! Once his eyes knew everything, and
gleamed in reflecting it, holding its image in a conscious
twinkle. To his rascal cousins he is something unnatural.
They feel as uncomfortable with him as they might with
the preacher, who being apprised of certainties has no
need to offer them to all and sundry but holds his
counsel out of sermon time. Gruffudd has no opportunity

for sermons, but they sense that he is always holding something back, like a schoolmaster in the holidays.

When Yfan straightens from a fleece to let out a great belch, a deep gassy performance that cries out for rebuke or imitation, Gruffudd doesn't even look up. Yfan stands with his shears poised and his belly flexed as if for recitative. He looks glazed, self-absorbed. It is the relish and finesse of conscious skill; the sounding of a note, like the organ's introductory reminder of the hymn, which is intended to alert, to encourage, to impress; a signal of weary endurance, of pleasures past and passing, of life lived to the full; a mild insult, an invitation to the interruption of work. It gathers in the stomach, an accretion like the lurching bubbles of fermenting beer in a casket. The mouth opens to acknowledge its imminent arrival, and as it passes upwards, air seeking air, the lips shape it lovingly, in a mock-solemn vibrato:

'Bey . . . ey . . . ey . . .'

Will sniggers, and Yfan bows deeply in response. But Gruffudd continues with his shearing as if he has heard nothing, and the stare of his eyes might contain either blankness or furious thinking, who can say?

Tuesday 18 August

Well might he mistrust the process of his reasoning, for reason would conclude that, for example, Uncle Huw is robbing the ewes. Cool as a cucumber he waylays them, brazenly throws them to the ground, ties their legs, reaches into their inside pockets, deeply into both sides, and even as they half-struggle against such an assault he has them out of their overcoats in an instant and sends them naked out of the shed.

What can it profit him? They have no silver, and no gold but in the blankness of their eyes. Their overcoats are folded inside out and stowed in the bag with all the others.

Wednesday 19 August

His intuition will tell him worse, for he has put the ram to the ewes and knows their complaisance. And why should a woman not be the same?

There are rams and rams, and some will not serve. But though there are barren ewes he has known none that do not take the reddle. Put them in that emerald room called hyfryd and soon enough their rumps are red. The field might as well be a whole village, for Maharajah Maharen will serve sixty ewes without loss of interest.

And what about himself, then, the amusing man? Has he some delicacy, like Mr Rhydychen who sits on the hillside filling a book when doubtless there is work to be done? Delicacy may be bred into folk as an excuse against those efforts they need not take, and is a sign to each other that they possess the wherewithal to avoid them. But some might compare it to a sickness.

Take Cousin Yfan, who has never had a day's illness in his life. His appetites are visible and audible, and by all accounts he scatters his seed freely.

But to be delicate in such matters, is it not deathly?

Thursday 20 August

But how should it be demonstrated? It isn't an argument with a seal, like a bottle that doesn't leak. It can never wear the visible sign of ownership and authority, be brought back writhing and protesting to be marked like the ewes that Will forgets. The raggedy boy brings her back into the shed where the mark is ready, dipped in the warm pitch, and in a minute she is once again irrefutably a Price possession.

Friday 21 August

Think, Gruffudd: isn't that confutation enough of your suspicions? He has his own mark of gold, warmed by her finger.

He resists. It could be a trap. She could be a stray.

But he really believes he is wrong. It is only his delicacy that defeats him, the sense that he has missed, and might now always miss, the conscious rights that were his.

He did nothing! And how can he not believe that the others did more? It freezes his blood.

When even the meanest slave who had dragged the stones that made the great Pyramids was dying, surrounded in his natural old age by children, and grandchildren, and great-grandchildren, something of desperation in his eyes, something of a wish to speak, made them attentive.

It is rarely reasoning that delivers judgement, but experience always makes a man wise. Even after a lifetime, when in a small way he has himself become a wonder, his ignorance will be apparent. It is both a surprise and no surprise, like the pattern that has long faded from a curtain, which is revealed when the lining is renewed.

The words are always in his head, uttered to his unwilling heirs, the coming days of his life: 'Is that all it was?'

The single sunflower at Uwch Hafotty, bent by winds in its infancy even in that corner of the yard that gave it shelter, tied up now with string like a bronze sign for the

82

summer's lodging, is in effect a greater wonder up there than the hanging Gardens of Babylon. If the heedless air had not taken it, then witless water would, for Yfan pisses on it every day at sunrise.

The last ewe is turned out again on to the mountain. The dogs lie in the shade, lolling their bright tongues, red as the lesson-marker that hangs over the lectern, wetter than that, but a signal for sitting. The men tie up the field gates.

Suddenly they are running. Will is ahead, his rolled shirt sleeves working like the pump. Huw was granted a start, but his hat flew off. The raggedy boy is doing well, for he doesn't stumble. Yfan is too fat. The dogs leap up and follow, with bright encouraging barks. For Gruffudd, who is somewhere and nowhere, it is a mockery, as though they enact the heart of his unhappiness. It is like a ghost of the wedding.

And similar games, with leaping and with horseshoes. The prize is a purse nailed over the door, with small silver for the wether's lost seed. Another ghost.

And in the evening of the ffest, his aunt and cousins bring in the weanling lamb, stewed in thyme and wild garlic.

Monday 24 August

This running towards the future in the confident belief that it is always there! The spirit in which Mausolus built his tomb is the spirit that bakes the cacen gneifio, for even tomorrow is as uncertain as eternity. Lads, take your prize! But Gruffudd turns to look again at the past. And the future will be nothing but crumbs, like the crumbs of the shearing cake.

Tuesday 25 August

Is there anything to which he can give his voluntary assent? Though reason tells him otherwise he would like a world where everything is entirely what it should be. The Temple of Diana is not the shrine of Juno.

Wednesday 26 August

No silver snatched off a lintel compares with the secure harbour of knowledge. No candle flickering over a pack of cards compares with a beam from the chamber in the hands of the Colossus, lighting the way for the spice ships.

'King of Hearts,' exclaims Uncle Huw in triumph, as if it were itself a barque long-awaited from the Orient. His slow pinching fingers gather and lift cake crumbs from the table to his mouth.

The cards are greasy with lanolin from the robbed wool of the ewes.

84

Thursday 27 August

In the morning the cards are still strewn on the table, uppermost a vermilion and ochre profile less noble than the Jupiter by Phidias, but a sign of comparable power and wonder, for it gained Huw the shilling won by Will in the racing.

Tales told of Mr Driscoll's grandfather winning sixty acres in a game of loo, and no pistols on the table either. And other legends. Win or lose (and every win is a loss for another) the truth of these negotiations is as nothing compared to the winning and losing of a future and a family.

A man may run for the rest of his life before losing a similar fortune, and who cares if it be true or not that he becomes a legend in his own lifetime?

Friday 28 August

You'd think there was nothing left to do, nothing to get up for, no reason not to stay up half the night and sleep in the morning. The slate is scratched all over with the story of loss, first Will and then Yfan. It is like a tombstone remembering each evening's dead hilarity, the luck first of the boy who could not be blamed, and then of Gruffudd, who could. And is, though it is not fair to blame the luck of a man who is not happy and therefore cannot enjoy it. Uncle Huw retires to his pipe, and Gruffudd builds a card Palace of Cyrus from the rigid forms of numbered slaves and defeated monarchs. Candlelight stirs in the spoons and the dog grunts in his sleep. The pasteboard triumph is only the claim of a moment, for the dog will wake to a scuttling cockroach and the candle will gutter. Huw will stretch and knock out his pipe against the grate.

Tomorrow there are walls to mend, and the cards are flat upon the table, the joke on Gruffudd's lips unspoken and barely thought of.

Saturday 29 August

A man builds a house stone upon stone. To begin with it seems no more than a wall, designed to keep everything within it from escaping. Soon he is unable to see over it and then it suddenly changes its purpose. Now it is to allow whatever is inside freely to get out.

Nothing is within that was not put there. This is called memory.

Sunday 30 August

Perhaps no one has the right to exist unless they have not been forgotten. To be seen on a summer's night, on the last Sunday in August, standing on the doorstep cleaning a pipe. There is the same claim against oblivion, the same assertion of habit to be recognised.

Monday 31 August

The walls are never quite closed. There are spaces in them like eyes that look always outwards to whatever it is that might be expected to occur.

Two figures that look across at each other.

Two pairs of legs crossed below the knee. Two pipes knocked out on two heels. Looking to left and to right.

Two closing doors.

Tuesday 1 September

This is the man's life. The looking out, the appraisal, the calm defensive gesture, the expectation. Then the turning back.

You have seen them in the village, fists in pockets, pretending to be front doors. Or smoking at windows, waiting to be greeted first. Or shouting.

Something is always going on behind them that they don't understand. They don't even know if they are meant to be in charge of it.

Then, when there are no more surprises, they will sit together on bleached benches in the sun, in a joy of tobacco.

Wednesday 2 September

How many chances are there? How many chances does a man get, before his gums meet? For Yfan it is something he will always put off. It is something to think about the following spring.

Send him to the bench.

And Will, trying all he can, but losing heart.

Send him to the bench.

They suspect that cousin Gruffudd cannot always have the luck. For he too would rather tie up a gate than untie a garter, he would rather burn his boat than burn a cake, he would rather tell a joke than take a gill, he would rather read than ride, he would rather remember than guess, he would rather wink than know, he would rather when than once, he would rather never than now. He would rather not.

Send him to the bench.

Thursday 3 September

As for his aunt, she thinks his mother brought him up to be too big for his boots indeed, for he laughs at no one's stories but his own, and those she can never understand.

With her wrist for a moment at her forehead, and pastry before her curling in cut shapes, she pauses in what she is saying and looks at him as though she has never seen him before. He is as pale as death for all the sun has roasted him, and only his fingers purple and straying to the bowl of bilberries on the table. Though she looks, he will not look back.

If he won't look back, why is he sitting there? If he will not talk why is he not with the others, pissing on the sunflower? What does he want her to say to him?

Is he asking her to tell him what is going to happen?

She has too much milking to do to look into the future.

Friday 4 September

And his uncle, who would like to see Will and Yfan married before he has to give them their land, thinks him a poor thin thing to have carried off that great staring girl, and what a mystery it is, with Will refused five times by girls with nothing to speak of at all, like pies with the fruit showing through. And Mair Hughes with her mane of hair who could stamp her foot in temper and break a spring from the hillside that would water Dic Hughes's sheep without his having to stir from behind his newspaper.

And what right did Dic Hughes have to hide behind a newspaper anyway? No one could tell when he learned to read, and nobody except him had so many newspapers. Did he buy one every week?

Gruffudd will be paid in draft ewes for his work

at Uwch Hafotty, but where do you suppose he will go now?

Saturday 5 September

Never say never, for the word doesn't belong to the imagination. It is useless in the picturing of likelihood, a denial of calculation. You can count for a star, and the tongue slows. But sooner or later, when you have tired of counting and your head thrown back is dizzy with the large still heavens rushing outwards from you in their motionless dazzle, and your eyes can no longer gaze everywhere at once, then . . . Then! The star you never thought to see marks the sky like the beginning of some patient tracing of a golden plan too immense to be continued. And everything is part of it. He particularly. And I . . . And you . . .

Perhaps he sees it too, wherever he is.

Sunday 6 September

I have never left you, though your days seem broken. At night, after searching for shooting stars, your pillow seems neither cool nor warm, but a turbulence; not like feathers but the tumbled earth of graves.

There is some meaning in this relationship between sky and earth.

Monday 7 September

You once heard a boy singing over a hedge, and it was as though he had not seen you but was singing a song of all young women who must beware of young travelling men. It was a song for the hour after the middle of the afternoon when the hands tie more slowly and the eyelids are heavy. You sat back on your heels and listened. And then there he was at the gate.

What meaning is there in such incidents? Does it now strike you freshly as a tale that might be told of your own travelling man?

Tuesday 8 September

Protection of a critical sisterhood; the power of survival and experience; free advice to the suffering; wonder at the strangeness of such a marriage. You have never been so visited by inquisitive kindness, walking gifts of buttermilk and early apples, tender words shadowed by crowing triumph. They come, all of them, so that they can guess what it is about you that has sent him packing. As if they didn't already know you from your girlhood, your brown knees mapped by brambles, your heavy black hair starred with burrs, striding on ahead, alone.

Polly has news of him. The ewe lambs have long been in the lower pastures. Huw Price has blacked up his market boots and Gruffudd has gone with his cousins to work on the new road below Pen-y-groes.

Wednesday 9 September

Or has he? Dandi Pugh stood him an ale in Caernarfon and brings you four shillings from him wrapped in paper. There is not a scrap of writing on the paper, nor any talk of roads from Dandi Pugh, who is of the opinion that the shillings are sheep money and nothing like all of it.

'A man may sell ewes in Caernarfon, yes, and buy them, too!'

What does *that* mean? And what does Dandi Pugh know of it?

Thursday 10 September

Pugh is full of righteousness, and protection of the innocent. His last words yesterday were a tease as he squared off your shillings on the table, moving each pair together and apart, together and apart with two fingers of each hand, like the dance with fiddlers.

'Four faces of the same man is a kind of wonder, Mair, and every one a sailor! North, South, East and West! A king may look to his dominions in every direction. William the Sailor King.'

Friday 11 September

The paper, unfolded, lies on the table. The nine panels of its folds at an easy relation with each other, like the moves of a ghostly game, eight to the circuit and one at the centre. For eight months thou shalt labour, and in the ninth thou shalt come before the divine awfulness.

Is this the correct interpretation? Hardly. The only interpretation involves the absence of writing and the silver obligation of an absent husband. The statement and the very person, both missing, the shillings doing a double duty.

Saturday 12 September

Polly once more, shown the shillings, as if to say: 'Whatever sin may be purchased in the back streets of Caernarfon, these four coins have played no part.' You believe she believes it, or rather, you believe that she believes you believe it, a convenient charity that lets you both eat in friendliness the biscuits she has brought you.

But rounds of brown are goodness always, and rounds of silver may in their time have been wicked.

In the evening Dandi Pugh appears again as if to explain how, with his dog quivering and looking likely itself to swallow whole any biscuits it might be given. You give it none, nor any to Dandi, either, who has his usual wisdom (or is it folly?) to impart.

Sunday 13 September

The manifest meaning suitable for Polly Jones is not the latent meaning that now haunts you, the foreboding difference between a shilling and a sheep:

Acknowledges the past. Belongs nowhere. Changeless possession. Deaf to dogs. Eats nothing. Fleece of silver. Gleams in moonlight. Hostage to hoarding. Immune to illness. Jaw unmoving. Kingly profile. Lost in a field. Many markings. Noiseless wealth. Odourless oof. Pride of the purse. Quickly spent. Regal eye. Silent at lambing. Two-sided. Unscarred by scab. Vain brow. Wage for workers. Expecting nothing. Yielding no yarn. Zero growth.

Monday 14 September

Now it is easy to imagine them all thinking that if Gruffudd is minded to come home he would not have sold his sheep for shillings, whatever pride it gives you in that sign of his support, a faithful packet of metal money, from wage-wanderer to wife. Would he not need his draft ewes to graze his own grass? What will he put the tilted fields of Nant-y-cwm to? Turnips that may rot through a wet winter?

You wander down to the wood with a knife and a basket, for russulas coloured as fairings, chipped like crocks. Water trickles below the mosses. When you return, your mother is at the cottage door. You were not yesterday at Saron. Twm has a bad tooth. She has yeast left over from her baking.

These now are practical days, with news for feelings. The weeping is done with.

Tuesday 15 September

There is concealment no longer, your dress let out like a secret. It is getting more like the size it should be, a thing that will have to be exposed. There is relief in the village, as at a visible sign of humbling, an opportunity for acceptance. The Mair who paced by in boots with a word for no one has been brought like a proud schooner to anchor, a hulk uncaptained. The new Mair is now to be protected and encouraged. The visiting sisterhood have done with irony and insinuation.

Megan is taking the Thomas girls on a gwlana while the weather is fair and there may be spare fleeces at the more generous farms. Old Mrs Davies wants to come wool-gathering, too, though last year she complained that she was beyond sleeping in barns for charity.

You look up from your threading. Strings of white slices for drying, each with its red or yellow line of cap, or the ash-blue grey of the Charcoal Burner, like petals.

'Yes,' you say. You will go, too. Not for the money (though who knows where the next shillings will come from?) but for the company. And to stir sloth.

Strings of them already hanging from the ceiling, like the solid mapping of a falling petal, the shape strangely repeated, solid in air.

Wednesday 16 September

Another reason to go is to avoid the attentions of Pugh, who never leaves your cottage but with the easy air and half-finished ideas of someone who will soon be back without any particular invitation. Though you hide your anger at him, or vent it on his dog, you blame him for the knowledge that feeds his sententiousness, information about Gruffudd that he has no intention of imparting, disclosures in general that do not concern him except as fuel for his irony.

You will go on Saturday. Megan will bring oatmeal, and flour sacks, light but strong enough for the wool. You are to bring lantern, candles, flint and tinder. Mr Thomas promises cheese.

Thursday 17 September

Here he is again, in the disguise of a fool. His coarseness is couched in elegance, for Dandi is the hand at a bidding speech, or verses at the front door, but it is coarseness nonetheless, as though a woman who has once seen what she should not see can never again think of anything else.

Widows of sea-captains, forever rounding promontories; widows of hauliers, whipping granite through unmelted passes; widows of itinerant preachers, shaming the parishes. Widows of the mine, widows of the pilgrims' road, widows of the hiring-fair. Plump widows, toothless widows, child widows, widows in actuality, stoking graves with yellow spring flowers and raking the granite chippings like ovens. All with lodestone in their hearts, the yearning for the male!

Friday 18 September

The Riddles of Dandi Pugh:
1. 'Pa ddau na anwyd a fuont feirw?' will make any maid blush who has learned that babies are not born out of navels, for navels are a sign that our mother and father did the deed. It is Adam and Eve who died before they were born, for they had no mother and father.
2. There are holes in the body through which the

future enters and holes in the body out of which the future is created. Which hole is closed upon the past?

3. What is the destiny of every woman? (No, it is not what you think. It is to be born of woman.)

4. What is the destiny of every man? (It is to ask riddles.)

5. How should a man know who to marry? (No man should marry.)

6. How should a woman know who to marry? (Jump overboard and marry the man who jumps in after you.)

7. 'Pwy fu farw cyn geni ei dad?' Isn't this where we began? You can say that it was Cain who died before his father was born, but we have heard of other fathers who thought their sons might be fatherless.

The navel is the seal and authority of the mother.

Saturday 19 September

The one riddle of Gruffudd Price: infinite stillness of soul, quiet wit, sturdy, thorough, trusting; but undercut by gulfs of suspicion, stubbornness, impossible hopes. The world must be perfect for him. If not, it is suddenly nothing. He is one of those men who live at a level from which they will forever be let down. Temper is one of his public vices, the obverse of his secret longing for perfection. There is no outlet for it in this situation. He brought it upon himself.

Before you go, you pick up once more the torn piece the shillings were folded in. Light from the window deepens the folds, still empty of the things written only in his mind, things difficult to describe. Why is there nothing written?

Every letter he might write is missing.

Sunday 20 September

On the first day you complete the parish fields with half a sack, perhaps three pounds, and turn away from the setting sun towards Pen-y-gaer, where you will lodge with Mr Thomas's cousin. Your thoughts are chains.

You and he are now like a chart of fresh heavens, an ever-changing and imaginary line joining two hypothetical points, the significance of which is pure speculation, though crucial. Your lives are linked like a path across a field, where the gate you entered and the gate you will leave from are neither of them known, though the journey is for the moment everything. You sense that you are like the opposed currents of one sea, whose waves advance on one shore at the very moment that they retreat on another.

This is the second of his missing letters.

Monday 21 September

Looking at the Thomas girls, you see that one sleeps with her mouth open and one sleeps with her mouth shut. It is like an illustration of the two essential parts of one bodily mystery: open, shut, open, shut, a movement in stillness to keep up the flame of the human spirit, an impulse of air as from invisible bellows, the divine nostrils breathing through the strangely similar faces. They make no sound, and their breasts hardly move. One mouth open and one mouth shut, as though robins would fly down with the first of the falling leaves and make them a forest blanket.

Have you yet thought that it might be twins? Doesn't it after all seem natural for there to be two, one for you and one for him? If he has thought of this himself you have no means of knowing. The question hangs in the miles of air between you.

This is the third of his missing letters.

Tuesday 22 September

'They say that every time you tell a lie you leave a little part of yourself in the place that you tell it.'

'Never!'

'Yes. That's what blushing is. When you tell a lie you feel that little bit of yourself trickling out of your cheeks. It's your small store of the truth leaking away.'

'Glennys tells lies all the time.'

'Not as many as *you*, bum-face.'

'We all tell lies to protect us from shame, but truly it's the lies that bring the real shame, isn't it?'

'My mother says that sometimes it's polite to lie.'

'White lies leave the lightest traces, to be sure, but what about the brown lies and blue lies? Like these, look, caught on these bushes?'

'Everyone knows that ewes are the greatest liars of all. Listen to their voices.'

Yes, listen to their voices, thin uncertain claims to possession of paths and offspring, quavering assertion of rights that are quite without basis. Are they not in this somewhat like men?

But where are his righteous claims? Where his sense of property? This is the fourth of his missing letters.

Wednesday 23 September

A chilly night in a barn not far from Glasfryn, with sucan blawd pulsing and stirring in a pot on hot coals and ash. A flint-struck spark has caught light wisps of hay and bits of wool, and sticks laid across soon light up, too. Dry dung now slowly imparts a glow, smoking badly at first but with only a thin faint odour of cow.

Warm spoonfuls, islands in milk. Canary sugar, shavings from an oak box, your small luxury.

Nodding off, with no comfort of arm or murmur of

admiration. No kiss at nightfall, no wrist on waist, laying claim or asking for attention, nostrils moving slowly in unison, in and out, with slow air passing across pillows, yours and his. Wax flaming in gusts, big shadows on walls.

On this, your fifth day of missing communications.

Thursday 24 September

Asleep when you wake, brow, nose, mouth and chin in a single line at an angled relation to each other, alike still and completed, like a trick at cards. Should twin girls be able to breed together, that would be an exclusion all right, keeping the whole world at bay! A purer posterity, a quintessence, whatever is common in their likeness distilled and working simply to its own end, in perpetuity.

But you are no bloom, to be so consummated and predicted. No one can point or gather, saying: 'This is Mair, and always will be, though dying and rising again in the course of seasons.'

It will be new, and its vigour knows it. It doesn't only belong to you. It belongs to him, though it is not him either. He must claim it!

This is the sixth missing letter.

Friday 25 September

The heaviness of the wool-sack speaks to you. Carried on your back it echoes the other fullness. However much is sold there will be some over to spin, and you will make of the spun wool a shape that is like the shape that it will be, itself a shape that will be like you, knitted bone and sinew of your own body's intentions to represent the mystery that otherwise would have no shape.

Your hand turns the wheel of the future whose invisible centre spins on his axis. You move, but he seems not to move. And now it moves, in response to voices that make music round a fire. And would move to his, too, were he here.

This is the seventh of his unsent letters.

Saturday 26 September

Now you are deep in it, no tracks for turning quickly back, no giving up. Born even now, in some freak circumstance, it would look like itself. You have reached the Pistyll of your gwlana, six notes of the unwritten song. Onwards!

Sing it in A for majesty, the expanded lung.

Sunday 27 September

Or B, key of the earth, unadorned ground-note of the sphere, thud of heart-beat and thunder of the waters.

Monday 28 September

Or C, key of containment, of cynefin, its pleasure in the habitat. You know it cannot stray, grazing in the sustaining liquids. And the sacks are nearly full.

Tuesday 29 September

Or D, mode of melody, consciousness of fate and the facing of it. What would be recognition in sight and wisdom in speech, and as it is, is stillness in the silence and in the night.

Wednesday 30 September

Or E, key of emotion and memory, that ponders every evening by the embers the sweet sadness of its experience. It does not wish to say much. One phrase is enough.

Thursday 1 October

Or F, the busiest key, the key of discourse and gossip. What news down there in the senseless dark? What coasting in on buoyant tides? What light dancing on rocks? What eagerness to complete the circle?

Friday 2 October

Or G, the key of all that is achieved like the clearest lit sky of the summer, crammed with their bright dust that appears as a severe book whose last page still waits to be read but which is already completely of your heart.

Tomorrow is home, the music always richest just after it has stopped.

Saturday 3 October

Did nights in the fields and byres bring any peace? Such times as the hay-harvest and the reaping have always put the heart where arms and back are busiest, linked in a line, passing hand to hand; put it in friends' care, dripping with sweat, the shared task between girls and wives. Where can we find whatever will link him and . . .

Returning in the darkness multiplies all that is missing, even the self that I address (with that circle at its centre which is the marriage sign and which I find I can't for a strange reason name).

This is the fifteenth missing letter.

Sunday 4 October

Coming out of Saron with your father and mother and with your hands folded over the Word that lies on your matronly belly (black as the night which it is intended to illuminate and just as severely enclosed in form as in colour) you feel yourself easily wedded by default to your family and to God. Restored, in effect, after dreamlike wanderings, to your old condition.

It is so at the best of times, because of the mother's memory, drawing you back in your condition to her condition that begot you, wishing without choosing to wish to share again the bringing forth. How much more so does Gruffudd's exile terminate your own: he could not leave you in this limbo of absence. But he has never said: 'Go back to them.'

This is the sixteenth of the missing letters.

Monday 5 October

What about that other little repository of wisdom, that baby-bible, does it have anything yet to say? It is similarly sized and spined, and if it has no language, at least (at least!) it has now its operative lungs and a nervous system to control its breathing and body temperature. And at all those songs around the vagrant fires of the gwlana it responded with movement, as if with the mazes of dance or a reaching for the mother's voice as the echo of her soul. How much of your crooning was a prediction of suckling? How much was simply a lament? And what of the father's voice, never yet sensed? What would a response to that signify?

This is the seventeenth of the missing letters.

Tuesday 6 October

If life at Nant-y-cwm had not become so much a habit (quite a new life, indeed, of only twelve weeks' standing given expeditions and absences, but belonging to you in a unique way of all the episodes in the life up to now that you have known) then you might have upped and gone.

You take no account of what may be owed to you, such as the gwlana money, and what you might owe, to Megan in the case of oatmeal, and pennies due to village supplies. Such debts will wait. The debt of all debts is his, the one that lays claim to a habit of his own, yielded when not begun.

This is the eighteenth that is missing.

Wednesday 7 October

Now you are hedge-garnering for a winter that you can't avoid, wherever you are. Today the fruit of the elder, already draggled where the beak probed before the finger. Tomorrow, maybe, the bramble if the Devil didn't notice them when he flitted by the other day, and left them alone. You are late for much that you expect to be plentiful. Even the rowan, often unregarded, now growing thinly, with tell-tale orange on the rock where chat or finch for a moment warily excreted.

Gruffudd, known to like the half-fermented liquor made from rowanberry and honey, might have an opinion, mightn't he, if he were here? You think of him when you gather, and wonder if your intention and forethought might find favour with him. You will get no reply.

The nineteenth letter.

Thursday 8 October

Busy with boiling and jars, you are surprised before noon by Dandi Pugh appearing again as a courier of the missing husband, carrying no shillings, nor any blank paper, nor any message as such. However, he is driving a flock of sheep before him, lordly and unconcerned, barely perspiring as a serious drover would, looking like a mischievous minor god in an old canvas, poking a rump now and again in an unconvincing manner, munching an apple.

Where are such fine ewes bound for? Nowhere beyond here, for sure. Affairs are looking up, indeed.

Wise boy Pugh, one finger beside his nose, a small smile saying less. Nine ewes driven in. Nine ewes already nibbling grass.

Missing in series, as before, if a sign of hope.

Friday 9 October

Now in a flood of light at dawn and a peaceable stillness at evening, with thistles casting long shadows in the fields, the landscape settles and breathes. Pans are simmering and pots are filling. Inside the cottage the smell of berries; beyond, the smell of sheep.

Dandi is mending the wall by the stream to keep them from straying into the kitchen garden. Has he been told to do this, or is it his own idea? Nothing is clear yet, so he might as well get on with it. You want him gone, but no matter. He is singing hymns.

This is the twenty-first missing letter.

Saturday 10 October

This is haf bach gwylhingel, St Michael's little summer. The swifts are gone, but the green woodpecker still comes each morning to the big ash tree. Sometimes his knocking is louder than the sound of stones lodged and shifted into place, where Dandi Pugh stands weighing them in his hands.

You would not call him a labouring man. His building of the fallen wall, like all he does, has too much the air of a performance. He bends with deliberation, slowly, with reluctance. He holds the boulder delicately, as though it were an animal. He stands with it, as though for admiration. Perhaps he really is going to turn it into a

109

rabbit? His back is straight. He hasn't taken off his hat, which has feathers in it. The late sun catches the lichens, ochre, fawn, rust, marking them with light, settling them in their positions. Dandi strokes the mossy back of the stone he has picked up, as though to find it a position like enough to its old one, so that it will continue to weather, and to harbour growing things.

Oh, but he can't make a wall like Gruffudd! The stones lie squarely and will not shift, but they do not easily follow the fall of the ground.

This is the twenty-second missing letter.

Sunday 11 October

Although it is a day of leisure, Dandi returns to finish the top layer of stones, stacked at angles like the strokes of capital letters. It makes a long, uninterrupted and meaningless sentence, or perhaps it has one meaning in the language of granite: 'Forbidden to sheep.'

Dandi is grateful for tea and stands on the front step holding the cup cradled in one hand like something he is about to cast aside.

He intends to come the next day to make a hurdle. Is this going on for ever? Have you lost a husband only to exchange him for a comedian? There is no contract for it, and even had there been you could never have put your name to it.

This is the next of his missing letters.

Coming again to the door for refreshment, he sweeps off his feathered hat to make it for a moment a bird shyly taking crumbs from the grass. He mimes his snuffing of your latest boiling with twitching nose, like a dog in the heather catching the scent of a rabbit. This prompts another riddle:

> 'Ladi den, den, gown ddu heb yr un hem,
> Calon o garreg a choes ben.'

He looks at you with his round face, the eyebrows nudging each other into a question. Who is this lady in the black gown without a hem, who has a heart of stone and a wooden leg? For a moment, though you know the answer well enough, you can think only of yourself, as though the riddle, like the shillings, the sheep and the hurdle, indeed, like Pugh himself, come from Gruffudd and have a particular meaning. Which of them has a heart of stone?

Oh yes, you agree airily. It is far too soon to be picking sloes, before the first frosts. But why not? They are plentiful, and your muslin well-purpled already, your pots scoured and waiting.

Pugh's eyebrows move in a contrary direction at this remark, as though to make another meaning of it.

'Come to me, lad of mine!' he warbles. 'The night is short.'

You turn and go into the cottage without a word. This is the twenty-fourth of his missing letters.

Tuesday 13 October

The chief ewe bears a remarkable resemblance to Mrs Price, with that look after chewing that is all about grim satisfaction and a slight sense of outrage. This is the one moment that passes for intelligence in sheep, lost when the jaw resumes its motion. Perhaps this new arrival is her spirit, in all respects a noted absentee since her son's defection. The absence seems like approval or connivance.

The tongue protrudes as far as it can go, the fingers waggle with thumbs in the ears. Mrs Price stares back. There is no response to this face, nor to a human effort at bleating. After a moment her head descends again, the lips seeking grass.

This is the penultimate missing letter.

Wednesday 14 October

His is the heart of stone; yours the heart of blood. The muslin drips from the rafters just slower than a human pulse, streaked like flowers. Soon it will contain nothing but stones and pulp, to be turned out like a dead thing, to dry to a husk in the yard, pecked over by the hens. The stoneware bowl echoes to the measured fall of sloe juice, secure in its capacity to contain it. Each drop punctures the liquid surface and is absorbed by it, the crimson circumference imperceptibly enlarging, the trembling unmarked dial of a steady fruit clock.

All afternoon slowing down, the only sounds its steady deepening drip and the intermittent fury of bluebottles caught in an old web in a sunny corner of the window-pane.

His heart to be cast aside; yours to settle to a new shape? While there is still summer he may come back. Haf bach gwylhingel. He must be coming back to manage the sheep. Hearts like fruit can grow again. Calon o garreg . . .

This is the twenty-sixth missing letter.

Thursday 15 October

And suddenly there he is. You were rinsing clothes, and now are coming up with buckets from the stream, the handles slightly squeaking with the weight and wet. Something makes you look up across your right shoulder, and there is Gruffudd coming down the hill.

Now that he is there, within sight of the cottage and to all appearances walking in no other direction, it is easy to feel that your skill in divination placed him there. How often have you looked up to the sky in time to see a falling star, or the flight of the green woodpecker, while your mind was busy with other things?

If the eye creates the world it scans, why can it not create the world it wishes?

It is a week since his sheep arrived, more than thirteen weeks since he left. This was time enough to stop wishing, but the sheep were a sign, and though what was now expected could not be predicted, it could be wished for again and in this way be begotten of the eye.

In the eye now is the full figure, the hat with the severe brim tilted back, the knapsack, the saunter, the staff, the new boots. The figure approaches. You put down the buckets. The figure still approaches.

Friday 16 October

The days you have lost are a good proportion of the days you have known each other. With your lightest cunning, the airiest intuition of careless nonsense that will sit uncomfortably in his mind with the irrefutable figures that you conjure for him, you point out:

1. £10 of the bidding deposited at 3 per cent interest with Mr Unwin's brother at the bank in Caernarfon.
2. 1s. a day for the 94 days of his absence comes to £4 14s.
3. Remainder of bidding (intact in teapot) comes to £4 8s. 6d.
4. Interest for three months on deposit comes to 1s. 6d. (not in hand).
5. 4s. sent via Dandi Pugh in folded paper without friendly greeting, words of contrition or statement of future intention.

6. £4 8s. 6d. plus 1s. 6d. plus 4s. equals £4 14s.

He doesn't see it at all. 'Where could I get a shilling a day from?' he asks. He doesn't seem impressed that the remainder of the bidding is still unspent. He is proposing to spend it himself, on more sheep. And the deposit, too, for that matter.

Saturday 17 October

Where has the demon gone, if it has gone at all? Is he in his heart truly sorry, but will not say so for pride? He seems now to be rejoining his life after the event. He has been lapped in the race. He has been lost for a season. He is ninety-four difficult unremembered dreams ahead of schedule. His humour is out-of-date. His stories are foreign history. His heart died in his old boots, and the new one has not yet been worn in. And he has a brooch for you, which mysteriously spells your name.

Sunday 18 October

When he came back he seemed easy to kiss. It was something that had to be done, so that when one of the buckets got in the way of your feet you simply kicked it aside. The water welled out over the grass heedlessly, though you kept in your tears, and while you had your face in his neck and shoulder and your arms round the tightness of his coat and the straps of his bottle and knapsack, you felt in his body a sigh and a yielding that spoke silently for all that he has not yet said.

As if, with weapons broken and supplies unforthcoming, two armies should face each other across the banks of a. river. There might be swimming and good-natured shouting, though the terms of a treaty were far from settled.

The walls of Saron bathed in evening light. Fresh flocks, and little Edwin shouting to the dogs.

Monday 19 October

These days are all walls and lacing boots and doors slamming, all that gets in the way of a remembered kiss. But you have his brooch to wear, the latest of his presents, the real present of his sorrow. It is like his touch. It places you. It has put you where you are, at the centre of all this activity, the filling of the Nant-y-cwm fields with sheep. You wear the graven word in its little flaggy capitals like a label.

But you are already at the centre of your own activity.

Tuesday 20 October

Out there in the fields the centre of activity is Maharajah Maharen. Cousin Yfan brought him from Pantypistyll in a cart, legs tethered, nodding from his creamy fur shoulders like Lady Newborough at the county show. Looking at him now, uneasy in his frozen strut among the thistles, you see what it is that makes him impervious to shame or exile, the deep swag of his mortal belongings, that tight bulk between his legs, thick with eager lamb-seedlings, that woolly powder-flask, that hanging flesh-bomb. Strange, you think, the nakedness of udder and the woolliness of testicle, how in the female the body is generously open and in the male closed in guardedness. Is it like that, will it be like that, with you and him? The father giving for his own purposes, the mother for the child's?

A naked man is sometimes as frightened as a naked woman. But the ram is half the flock.

Wednesday 21 October

The Maharajah is as willing and unwilling as a man can be. The ridiculous eyes are vacant with the deep incompetence of lust.

If it were a man indeed, it would be making jokes like Dandi Pugh.

Or standing in the thistles of his mind, like Gruffudd.

But the men must arrange things so that there is co-operation. Ladies, ladies, will you for a moment interrupt your tea? Will you come into my parlour at the dogs' insistence? With little skittish stumbles and nervous glances, while the hurdles are tied against your retreat?

And the reddled monster stands there in his profile and

on his dignity. And takes a mouthful or two to keep up his spirits.

Thursday 22 October

You are cutting bread for them all, Gruffudd and Edwin and Dandi, for still they have not gone. Dandi in seniority and self-esteem taking the settle, and little Edwin content with the barn, for there is more wall to shore up than anyone thought and the more unwilling of the ewes are escaping freely into the oak wood and stumbling across the stream, in order to avoid the now insistent Maharajah.

You hold the loaf to yourself like a second child and saw off the rounds as determinedly as if they were sections of Dandi Pugh's neck.

They are calculating.

'One hundred and forty-seven days,' says Gruffudd.

'Two hundred and fifty-two days,' you think to yourself.

'Five months forward and five days back,' says Dandi Pugh.

'Nine months forward and for ever,' you think, holding the knife.

Friday 23 October

This vast authority, requiring submission, is a mere quirk of nature. It is showing-off, the aggression of the vulnerable. You'd think, wouldn't you, that a horn (for example) would be most effective as a sharp length extended to the front, like Uncle Evan's bayonet above the chimney-piece at Ty-bach with which Taid once performed graphic thrusts and withdrawals before Nain cried into the crempog and told him to hang it up again. You have seen a horn like this in a picture of the least aggressive creature imaginable, the unicorn with its trusting head in the lady's flowery lap. This is not nature. Nature is devious, and turns her horns into a great parade of nonsense, curling and tapering like something blown by the band, hollow as a brandy-snap, ridged like a sea-shell, hard as a headache. They are like a wig turned into handles, hardly a weapon. The tip is an afterthought, like cream.

But there you are. The ram has to fight sideways, but hopes he won't have to fight at all. He just wants to be admired.

Saturday 24 October

When the man is delivered, he is saddened beyond measure. He is vacant, completed, an empty vessel, with as little to do as the Maharajah. When the woman is delivered, she is full of joy, for what she has become she both is and is not. One has become two.

This is the text you carry in your head. Only in the contentment of his return can you now judge the better contentment of your fulfilment.

The little mimic occupies its place of being. Now it is one with its wet house.

Sunday 25 October

The Maharajah has served, and served his purpose. He will be removed in state. The whole episode was clearly embarrassing, and on at least two occasions a voice in your left ear told you to fling a handful of knives and whisks about the room. You did not do so because of the presence of Dandi Pugh and little Edwin. There is something about Dandi Pugh's vertical eyebrows and drooping eyelids which requires a response in words rather than knives. You are outnumbered by the uncompleted with their sculpted sentences of theory and their interference with the means of subsistence (though little Edwin hardly counts as he can do little but fart).

In Saron, perhaps for the first time, you consider your image of God. You have had occasion enough to understand the failings of fathers, and are beginning to imagine the perfection of the unborn.

Monday 26 October

For the moment the great success of the divine parodist is to have turned upside down, which is, after all, the right way up. Once you stood on your head with your feet against the kitchen window-sill and gazed at the enormous harvest moon until it seemed that your feet belonged down there after all, on that queer wistful lopsided face, and that you might even jump back, pushing the whole weight of the earth away and up until it was as far away as the moon.

But the earth is too heavy to push away and the moon too far to jump down to. It would be as difficult as being born.

Tuesday 27 October

Not doing the impossible, what can that be? Nothing much. Not doing the difficult? A commonplace. What is the difference between the difficult and the easy? A short step. The hunted stride of failure that always seeks the shade of shame.

He knows there are blessings within his grasp, and of his making. He wants you to make it all right.

Wednesday 28 October

The life of prosperity for a man and a woman is the telling of sheep and the setting of cheese. It is knives lying still in a drawer, and whisks too. It is the creed of the Unwins, its tenets precise as museum specimens.

One considered deafness; one absent smile; one moment otherwise engaged; one automatic glance; one shared misunderstanding; one eager distraction; one patronising word; one forgivable self-absorption; one look elsewhere; one distracted dream; one unlucky truth.

The cycle is repeated. It is well under control.

Thursday 29 October

At pilnos you wish you had not come, for they are all there with their veiled talk and secret knowledge, worse than men after all in making the jokes that should be only men's.

The peeled rushes lie in rushlight like an image of the self-devouring cruelty of time. You think of the whole world running down or using itself up. Some of the things you do will never sustain you even for a tithe of the time it takes you to do them. Stealing blackberries to eat while gathering. The ewe's whole life is a meal. Illuminating the creation of light, the taper burning while you dip new tapers. Amen.

While from the corner comes the laughter of Sally and Hefyd as they sing to the tune of 'Hyd y frwynen', the length of the rush, snipping to a span that will portion a winter evening into its tasks.

Friday 30 October

How many times since his return have you said something to him, halfway between a question and an assertion, to link him with the child? You have put his hand on it, and he has looked at you as though his hand were on a book whose shut pages he could never read. All you want is for him to swear on it, as on a testament that he knows well enough not to read through first. It has to be believed in, and he has to say so.

And how many times since his return has he said something to you, halfway between an answer and a pacification that might satisfy a court of law, but would never satisfy your heart?

Undressing in the rushless dark.

Saturday 31 October

E nding is something that has started as soon as you begin, something that is never quite finished. But what of those like Gruffudd that never seem able to begin? The world is their amusement. They are ready, but they stand apart, not quite able to believe it. They live their lives like understudies. What they need, to detach them from their detachment, is something like a revelation. And this is what we are talking about here, him and it.

Once this has got going, it can conclude with dignity. There is little enough time, after all. More than half his span, he might say, but where has it gone already? It might be less than that, which would still seem long enough, but the last inch of taper burns quicker than the first (hyd y frwynen!) and when your body is ash there is no cutting a new one.

Or is there? When your own pilnos comes, will this within you not be a new life for dipping and burning? Freshly peeled, and sealed with the wax of the spirit?

All this you think as you make the hel solod as you have seen your mother make them. Soul cakes for the dead, authority to pass safely through purgatory. The dead who come to mind this Hollantide.

Sunday 1 November

In the night they pass in the double darkness of your shut lids: Uncle Evan, whose harp was lost but whose bayonet mysteriously survived; wild Cousin Owen, whose gun went off when he tripped over a heather-root at the edge of the bog below Llanpaen; Little Bell who never came back from sea. They have become only the shapes you can make of them. Evan a paler version of your father, though you do not think you ever saw him; Owen the mere ghost of a kiss which you can still feel, it being such a surprising area of skin for one to be placed; Little Bell a sighing sort of nothing, like the congregation of the waves praising the solid world at Parsal beach.

Do they miss their bodies, the dead? Or might they after all be glad to have become what they mean?

Monday 2 November

There are nights when you think you can almost hear the sea, though it is a mile off. The globe of your belly contains its own land and its own sea, turning and turning in the dark. Does it move at all to his star? Does it still steer by his command? You see the Pole Star there through the skylight, sharp in the frosty night. You are balanced in the bed now, weight for weight, and it keeps you at a guarded distance.

Tuesday 3 November

In the bed this morning, on his side, the disobedient stains of imaginary populations. Pwy laddodd un rhan o bedair o drigolion y byd? Who killed a quarter of the world's population?

Wednesday 4 November

The body's compulsion, its leaning, tilting, filling, is a kind of hydraulic performance, but for the mind in attendance it is the lurch and settling of a magnet. It is a force that is either there, or not there. What does it know of ghosts?

Thursday 5 November

His roles:

To be lord of nothing but acres, to be skilled in the filling of time.

To be captain of certain cures, to live from hope to hope.

To be counter of kingly faces, to long for the loss of labour.

To be master of the magnet, to lean across the void.

Friday 6 November

And yours:

To be servant of the seasons, to keep the house of the flesh.

To be follower of the fold, to learn to die in the dust.

To be searcher of lost light, to feel the dredge of the dark.

To be mistress of the waters, to hear the lap of the tides.

A Skin Diary

Through the pane, the star. What is neither in nor out? What two died who never were born? Is the life in your hands? Is it his gift, freely given and taken? Or is it a riddle that neither of you will ever understand?

Suppose the sky made the sea's noise? Or louder, because more of it, though further?

At night, emptying the chamber, you stand despite the frost beneath the sky's arched depth and distance, thick with dust and light. Why does it somehow feel heavy? When you turn up your face to it, it seems to press down on you with an unheard thunder.

As though the heavens themselves were waiting to bring you to birth.

When you climb the stairs again to his half-sleeping body you want to take him outside to show him, but you do no more than calm his stirring. He is dreaming some comedy, some little triumph of civic importance, of making a good impression in a difficult situation. You might mistake his muttering for a torture of guilt at leaving you to fend for yourself for months on end, and you might then wonder why you think you need him at all.

Except that his shape and smell speak of all that you

ever wanted from him and expect to want again, the slyness, the marrow of him, the insinuating flesh, the nerves of him, the trembling, like a dog that has scented the darkness.

Monday 9 November

For now, you are resigned to the other comedy, of keeping house and keeping sheep. It is all an experiment, with too little history. You feel life to be a pageant of exchanges – between man and animal, between man and woman, between woman and child. The roles are handed down, misheard, misunderstood, nothing written down, everything a mixture of the instinctual and the reinvented. And the pageant is never put away for a season. It goes on all the time.

Tuesday 10 November

He is curious about it, and hardly knows if he needs permission or not to touch. All his improvisations are dictated by the mind, not the body, so that the instinct which might issue in a reaching hand all too often turns into a contorted joke. Or a silence of self-hatred. Or a change of subject.

'Do you fancy a game of cards?'

Wednesday 11 November

How can you tell what is forbidden? You might well want a high drama rather than a low pasteboard farce, this game he played with his cousins, taught you in a friendly spirit, though you know it already. Perhaps he really thinks you know nothing at all? What does he imagine women *do*? He plays as earnestly as if he were at market.

Thursday 12 November

Each night he is closer as it gets colder. Some part (a knee, a hip) does not move away when it finds itself touching. You have to be as cautious as with a bird with a broken wing, rage draining into patience, tenderness suspended.

And yet you do not know if you should refuse him, were he to love you.

Friday 13 November

Can he take at least the same interest in it as he takes in the sheep? Or is it not real to him, not itself at all but merely your shape? He knows about dysentery, braxy, black disease, pulpy kidney, struck: what would he make of underinflated lungs, the alveolar surfaces covered with

129

a glassy hyaline membrane? Awake all night, listening to the hard and rapid breathing?

He can't imagine it.

Saturday 14 November

'Blessings on you, my children!' cries the irritating Dandi Pugh, waving his stick in the air as if to stir the mist as he would stir his flummery.

He passes by frequently, in the guise of benevolence, but you suspect that it may be because Gruffudd owes him money. For there have been more sheep, and the fields are full. Eighty sheep indeed, and more.

It seems clear to you, despite the broken-toothed smile which beams on you directly, that the blessing is reserved in Dandi Pugh's mind for the sheep.

Sunday 15 November

What does the village think? That he might leave his wife but that he would not leave his sheep? In Saron the word is predictable: the good shepherd rejoices in finding the lost sheep. Where does it say that the good shepherd rejoices in finding the lost wife? And what about the good wife finding the lost shepherd?

Nodding to Mrs Unwin, making promises to Evan Williams, shaking hands with the preacher, promising to cut Twm's hair, as only you can do it. Mrs Price even speaks with your mother. Gruffudd speaks with your father. The wind speaks with the graves.

Monday 16 November

The conditions of peace are that both sides shall maintain it. Every little article drafted and signed, concessions made, memorials visited. On the dresser still is the blown egg of Easter, with its twin red hearts like a pair of aces that can't win a trick from each other. The stone in his heart must melt now that his demon has been dispatched. If will and wit can do it, they must! If the favour of the darkest, handsomest, angriest young woman in the parish can be relied upon, he will rely upon it! There is nothing else for it. Otherwise his mother would say: 'I told you so.'

Tuesday 17 November

Trying the pickled hazelnuts to see if they are taking to their Egyptian half-life, you remember Dafydd Thomas. It is well over a year now since you told him that all was over between you. When he stood up, you stood up too, because you could never believe he was as tall as you and you needed to tower over him to dismiss him. The hazelnuts were forgotten and fell from your apron. You expected defiance, remonstration, criticism of Gruffudd. You expected to be grasped and kissed, or grasped and shaken. But he nodded, didn't he, and whistled to his dog, and the dog, so eager to be obedient and to be loved for it, came scampering through the trees and was tousled as a reward. Dafydd knew when he was bettered. Why does Gruffudd not see this? Did he want the child to be Dafydd's so that he could suffer? Dafydd, who had no idea at all how to get his hands into a dress, even if he whistled for it all day long!

Wednesday 18 November

What a trouble to get in! You would think the Tylwth Teg minded it, and were put on guard to protect you. Instead of as it is, them wanting to be in there themselves, nosing in crannies, sailing in sluices, rubbing, tickling, setting the air buzzing with curiosity and fainting. Perhaps that's just it. Every hair alive with the fair folk, making spears bristle as though with righteousness, the neck crawling, the eyebrows lifted, the forehead a watchtower. Every linen lintel, every neck hem or wrist pucker, every woollen tunnel severely populated. Every ache, every eagerness, a fairy's stroke. There is deep blood in their hoarded cellars, there is seepage, and chuckling. The buds are heavy, nodding, ridden by the folk.

Does he know it? He has never seen them, so could not tell whether they are puritans or rioters. But all they perform, they perform for him. The stage is his.

They have done their work, but some little imp,

some dozy straggler, forgets this now and then and half-recollects his moist instructions. It can bring a sigh to your lips in the deepest part of the night.

Thursday 19 November

Scything the thistles, he mutters: 'This should have been done in the spring.' But who should have done it, little Edwin or himself? His mind was on other things, after all.

The thistle is a tall soldier, and you watched its seed float on the air all summer. It was like the hillside making love to itself. You might have scythed it away yourself. Did you think of it? Did you notice?

Polly Parry, once she ceased to believe that children were born from the navel and that young girls slightly dizzy with lemon punch could be impregnated by sly kisses of seedcake, had much to say about the Rector. Dear Rector, sturdy man! Easily abashed, but usually there with his confession.

There were many versions of the Rector, said Polly. Sprightly Rector, rubicund and unreproved; lolling Rector; Rector nodding in his nap; Rector just before tea, expecting the maid; Captain Rector, angry at an insult; Rector bobbing and weaving for the fight; smooth Rector, insinuating Rector, Rector practically talking; Rector weeping; Rector laughing; Rector pretending successfully to be a little man; Rector elbowing to the front; Rector slipping away; Rector encouraged; Rector eager to be revived; Rector entirely lost.

The thistles are bound to come again.

Friday 20 November

Now you are almost there! What is in and out, and is neither in nor out? What do we send our bodies out into the world to do for us?

There is a moment when your eyes meet and for once he does not look away. The smile is a rueful smile, but it is a smile nonetheless. What does it say?

It says: 'I want to be a window into a room I have never myself seen. I want to let in the light, even though I am afraid of what I might find there. I need to believe that you will not be afraid. I want you to lead me into my own soul.'

Saturday 21 November

The roses and the lilies are eternal, like the night sky. Your bed is a wooden stage on which all farce and all tragedy have been and will be played. Dressing hurriedly in the cold, you sense that you are simply waiting for your role to be written.

Gruffudd is already in the fields. Something not perfectly remembered or understood makes you do something you have never done: you stand at the window

134

and shout to him. He turns promptly, and waves. And stands for a time, looking. He is just too far for you to see the expression on his face, but you keep your hand in the air in greeting. This unaccustomed parley brings back what it is that you had forgotten: a whisper in the night, half-woken, intimate words and intimate touch, words of forgiveness, the touch of possession.

Sunday 22 November

In the light that falls from the chapel windows are many heads remembering such moments, some worse, few better. Mr Thomas's neck is wrapped up, as though the boil beneath were precious or for sale. Megan has a new shawl. Dafydd Williams drops his hymn book. Mr Unwin contrives as usual to sing louder than anyone else. But there is much that is not seen, not sung or said.

Afterwards, the mysterious sharing is continued in a purely social liturgy.

'When is she due, Mrs Hughes?'

Monday 23 November

How did it happen? Almost overnight you have settled into the life that imagination once predicted for you. His hands have taken their gift, and grasped the globe of his future. He has felt its hidden inhabitant and knows that the future is true. There is no trick.

You have received the wanderer again in your arms.
You have felt all that could never have been written
in the spaces of the nine folded squares, and felt it as
a simple answer in a riddle too complicated even to be
asked. There is no trick.

Its heart beneath his hands, his beneath yours. The
restitution will be complete when your heart lies beneath
its hands.

And it will look like him, after all.

The world has cost you nothing but your part in it. On
this frosty night there is one last riddle which you speak
to your unborn child as it moves in its shadowless cave
gulping your waters:

> 'Gwaun las, lydan
> A da Pantwhiban,
> Morwyn Ben'r aur,
> A gwas Pen'rarian.'

You stand in front of the thing that is neither in nor

out, and watch the cattle of Pantwhiban herded across the sky under the care of the servant of the silver head.

Friday 27 November

Night after night in the moonlight, as tonight, the skyline of his sleeping face. Night after night the sheetfolds and blanket bulges that become the climbing places of girlhood, the hill of his chest, the lonely dare, the bushes, gathering and giving, with liberal hand. Fingers curled that have strangely gripped, breathing steadily now, the Rector vanquished who ranted in his pulpit of roses and lilies, singing 'Hyd y frwynen'. And he has been raised from sleep.

Saturday 28 November

Being is no excuse for anything. It doesn't need to be. It has no decisions to make, nothing to regret. Everything it is, is what it does, and what it does it does without anxiety. Don't you understand this now? There are times when you will know that you are indeed yourself: held by the heels, reaching for eels; looked at in a particular way, across a hawthorn hedge; full in the acorn-loins of your last month. But to be yourself without knowing it! That is possibly the privilege of your bold paddler, the salt acrobat, the trapped tumbler, who has not yet come to its senses. Now is the time for silent speaking. You, as promised. And it. And I.

It is like a table across which we might understand each other. Or a horizon, that holds flag or features crucially indistinct. The treaty will be joy.

Sunday 29 November

Do you remember your frozen handstand and the moon larger than the earth you pushed away? You are that earth now, as your satellite wobbles into being.

You thought that you knew it had become itself. You thought that you knew when it had become itself. But that moment is always mysteriously imminent. It was you once. It was him once. You both came together again in time to acknowledge it. Now you will both in your very different ways have to stand aside to allow it to demonstrate that truth itself. Inevitably there will be regret.

Monday 30 November

Ask me if I'm relieved. Ask me who I am. Speak to me if you can. Or do you not yet know how to? The relief is mutual. Think of all that you do and have done, all that was simply waiting. The dripping and cutting of cheese, the peeling of rushes, the unlatching of wool from thistles, the threading and drying of blewits and penny buns, the cutting of Twm's hair while he puffed his cheeks and sang:

> 'Gorff wys ennyd
> Cyn dych wefyd
> I'th belydrog lys.'

(No, you'll not leave him, or at least not grieve him, for you'll cut his hair for many a year yet, and make him an uncle into the bargain.) Think of all that has been spun, repaired and preserved. It is as though, with the world about to change altogether, you are vainly trying to keep it in at the edges like a pebbled bulwark of sand. The tides sing in the whorly shell you found at Parsal beach, and Twm sings, with his ear at your belly:

> 'Mae y teithio
> Wedi 'th flino.'

Yes, you are weary, and the journey is a long one.

Tuesday 1 December

This is the month of the birth. This is the month of rain. The wind drives it all night against the slates, and the surges sound like cooking or burning. In the morning it is still there, a curtain you can never draw back. The eaves are melting. Drip, drip, drip.

Wednesday 2 December

There are moments when you can't think how it will ever get out, though you have seen animals enough. But it's a wonder they don't have to break you open like a hazelnut. Mr Unwin once grew a pear in a bottle and exhibited it at the Show, basking in clear liquor like a specimen.

You wish it were over.

Thursday 3 December

True wonder is reserved for the recognised. Standing by the stone at sunset, you see what you have seen many times before: Echo Valley, the crags where the goats stare, the sweep of the slopes to the sea, the distant wrinkling of the sea lit up like linen, the long coast of the island, the still mountains. These familiar shapes now seem both strange and doubly familiar: the rise of Penllechog, the surge to Gurn Ddu, the bulk of Gurn Goch. It is your shape, predicted for as long as you have known them, predicted since the Creation, for all that.

What would the mountains give birth to?

A Skin Diary

Friday 4 December

The little clothes. The shawls. The bonnets, like peonies.
Tiny stitching, like a spell at the breast to keep a soul
from fluttering away out of its new body. Nightdresses,
smelling of custard. Pride of the designing animal.

Saturday 5 December

The offerings come from all sides, tempting providence, you
say. Polly has made woollen boots in tight ribbed stitching,
graced with ribbon. They are tiny things, more like egg
cosies. From the feel of the feet under your ribs, something
more like Gruffudd's buckled leather might be necessary.

From Taid, a cradle that he has made, sturdy enough
to carry its occupant safely forward on the treacherous
flood of its sleeping life. Perhaps, you reflect, this is how
you inherit the dreams of your ancestors. Nain gives you
a rare kiss. And you all sit down to tea.

It has a firm enough grasp now to take the tiller.

Sunday 6 December

All is ready now, but you feel like a pressed crew that has
not left harbour. How many more Sundays, for the hopes
and endearments, and the automatic enquiries, always to
your mother rather than to you:

'How long will it be now, Mrs Hughes?'

A Skin Diary

Monday 7 December

Whose is the decision? Where the hand that decreed the precise term? No one will say, not even toothless Mrs Scabbard, who turns up on this drizzling Monday morning to see the lie of the land. She has been the first to set eyes on most of the parishioners under forty, including you and Gruffudd. For this reason, although he is seated in the parlour when she arrives, he makes an excuse and goes out into the rain, not knowing at first quite what to do. To him she is part of a mystery that is beyond his wish to fathom. She seems to come more out of nature than ceremony, and not for her own satisfaction, or else it would seem like charity.

He leaves you with her as an accomplice to her extraordinary project. Her moist grin is at once conniving and excluding, as if to say: 'We are in much the same business, you and I, but you have done your work; now I must do mine.'

He thinks she may be a witch.

Tuesday 8 December

Wisdom, toothless or not, might suggest that it would be more prudent to remain celibate. Those who have never so much as peeped into the Gardens of Delight are proud of the pure path they tread. Their neighbours are in awe of them, as of some rare bloom that will never be seen again.

Wednesday 9 December

The greatest justice done to a person has nothing to do with rewards, not for purity, generosity or skill. Nor with punishments, as for social derelictions or creative evil. These things done or undone, these qualities exercised or not, belong to the miscellaneous chances of human life, incidental characteristics of the corporate organism. But it is just that an individual should come into being, and for nothing else can that individual give unqualified thanks. The rest is his responsibility.

You are an agent of the significant gift, the primary value, the minting of a coin that may be spent anywhere. And the final account is beyond calculation.

Thursday 10 December

You have endured jealousy, thinking it despicable for the most part. But somewhere inside you is a crumb of recognition that perhaps you have been too free with your favours. And if Gruffudd has a reason particularly to hate or fear Dafydd Thomas you don't know of it, and I'm not going to tell you.

In fact there is not much that I can tell you, since you are barely aware of me at all. I hover at the edge of your inner consciousness, and only when you abstract yourself from the daily world of surface and succession can you yourself send out your slight signals.

You have been asked for forgiveness, and given it. What was his crime? He sulked. Did he neglect you? He knew you could look after yourself. Did he have any reason for sulking? He was father of a child without knowing it. He did nothing! This is not impossible, and is perhaps worse than conscious fathering which is all satisfaction in the process and little in the consequence. What compensation? Joy in the offspring. What disadvantage? Exclusion from parturition. What future for Gruffudd? I can't tell. What future for you? I can't see beyond days.

To that topsy-turvy explorer of inner space you are both an unknown cause. Soon you will be a known convenience. In the ordinary course of things this arrangement will prove of mutual benefit.

But what about love?

What, has it lost its thumb? What are those frantic movements, then? And that kicking again, against your ribs? Putting your hand there in passionate alarm, you feel you might almost grasp its foot, and nearly do so. The fandango is interrupted. Or is it a standing-still race, suddenly won? Or lost?

The last shearing is finished. The walls are tight. He is

waiting now for winter, and then for the lambing. Five months forward, five days back.

Sunday 13 December

So the words of the angel were true: 'Gocheled pob merch dawel' and the rest of it, a warning to quiet girls who find themselves cuddling a lad on his travels. But travelling is a manner of speaking for the ever-restlessness of all young men, and you were never a model of quiet, either. Moley Mair, the terror of the village, has become a bearing woman, with the stillness forced upon her, the patience and pain of duty. And Gruffudd takes his sidling orbit about you. You are his sun, though he never sings songs to that theme, morwyn Ben'r aur, maiden of the golden head, though maiden no more. If he sings at all, he sings to his stones.

Monday 14 December

Mrs Scabbard requires respect, and truly you should not laugh at her, for she is no witch and her very own daughter is in service at the Plas with Mrs Driscoll. But the information she has about (among other things) your secret parts is scarcely to be believed in, and requires much thought. Just now Mrs Scabbard is more concerned with vessels household than with vessels corporeal, and you are relieved to respond obediently to her inventory. All is in order.

Tuesday 15 December

Do you quite hear me yet? I am the voice that tells you what happens, but I have another part to play, one you will come to know well.

The closest word you silently utter is when a hand is laid on, as again today with your mother. As the implied blessing flows strangely backwards, you look up and catch her eye and just for a moment you understand.

Wednesday 16 December

You need not worry about your virtue, Mair. Desire is a device that comes without instructions, and from the beginning you have known without knowing. Your feelings are soon to be given embodiment, and desire at last will find its shadow.

Thursday 17 December

Now you are easily tired, but out of an exhilaration coloured by penance you find more and more to do.

Quietly, Gruffudd takes the knife from your hand and sits you down in the comfortable chair. And today he makes the tea.

You remember Mrs Scabbard's riddle: 'Beth sydd yn canu wrth ei grogi?' It seemed a perfect image of joy and endurance in suffering, so that you laughed out loud at her and she laughed back at you so broadly that you saw very particularly what a complete absence of teeth there was in her mouth.

What sings if you hang it? What indeed? Your mind could only envisage the supreme hero, and an articulation so absolute that it might be the one human call to outwit death. Something that old Mrs Scabbard with her many secrets might know too. The secret of innocence.

'Beth sydd yn canu wrth ei grogi?'

Why, a kettle, of course. It was Mrs Scabbard's way of asking for a cup of tea.

Friday 18 December

Now your preparations to come into your reward are almost complete. From Mrs Price the use of the trap to fetch Mrs Scabbard when needed (a sedate and proper consideration), from your father a ham (a homely thought), from your mother the offer to stay and help after the birth (once you would not have wanted it, but now you do), from Twm an insistent need to know what it is to be called (you have not decided).

And behind all this, subdued but unignorable, and as the days go by acquiring a mounting poignancy and drama, the irrelevant preparations for Christmas.

Inaugurating the ham, Gruffudd sets a place for Morus Trawsfynydd. This hospitable expectation of Morris from over the mountain, which Taid in his time has facetiously performed, is not unknown to you. Morris may say nothing and eat less, but the space reserved for him is a memorable welcome which lends cheer to the meal. Your story doesn't need such space as yet, but I take it as his awareness of your time, and of a sense of something missing. Like all true piety it requires neither explanation nor acknowledgement, but gives direction to the spirit.

No Saron today. You had wanted a final blessing but this morning you can't get yourself down the stairs. Your sense of divinity is, however, as provisional as of Morris the eternal guest. Your bed is now the stage for a different kind of epiphany, and what I whisper in your ear is too private to be told.

Monday 21 December

The plaintive sounds of the sheep from the fields below, distant and less distant, map the unseen path of a man coming up from the wood towards the cottage. You know it is Gruffudd, but have no means of knowing what he has been doing. When his head appears round the door, you know you have been dozing. There is a voice in your head still which you understand to be a means of linking one state of being with the next, a mapping of disjointed time as the sheep's disturbed interjections are of space. You are adrift, with only the absolute authority of your struggling cargo to guide you. Your freighted journey, for so long a trust, is now a form of worship.

Tuesday 22 December

This is a record of days. On every day some things are begun and some are finished. Cais ddoeth yn ei dyddyn, the rites of daily life wherein the wise man is to be found, for there is the only contentment. Expecting at any moment to leap into the trap to fetch Mrs Scabbard, he diverts himself with red oxide. What a time to be painting the front door! It is his small challenge to providence, though in the afternoon an unhelpful drizzle sets in.

In the night you cry out, and who knows what the word is? It might be a greeting or a warning. Something in between, perhaps, or the intuition of a name. If it is, it isn't one that is known, and he laughs you gently back to sleep. Through the skylight is the astounding radiance of a full moon, like an uncovering, and he doesn't sleep again.

Wednesday 23 December

Now it has had enough, its temple at the bone like an egg in an egg-cup. This is its irresponsible decision. Its days are up. It will present its case. It will appear in person. It will not wait any longer.

Gruffudd harnesses the trap.

Thursday 24 December

What is all this life and light? I'm going under, under and over. You're blinding me with a world I didn't think I wanted, a world where everything is the word that says it is and where there is a word for everything. I have tracked you for so long that I know your worthiness inside out. I wanted you to say: 'Yes, I am ready for you. I know you, too!' But days intervened, and the blank bright busy world of dailiness. I have it by heart now, but of course I shall have to unlearn it. I must unlearn everything. I'm going under. At last I am being it. And once I am it I shall have to become ignorant to be born. You have barely known me till now, and will take time to find me after. There is a word for what I am, but no one has learnt it yet.

Friday 25 December

Will this go on for ever?

You have never felt pain like this. You are bearing down on your refusal to accept it. Your mind has shrunk to a point of furious concentration, a tiny point, within which our strange transaction can be made. Don't you know the word yet? Don't you know my name? Take me! Take my knowledge of days to yourself, because I shall have them all to learn again. Take all that I know and give me the rest of your body. Let me stand in the night and cast a moonlight shadow!

This was my holiday with you, the closest I shall ever be. And the pain will take you straight to heaven. Maybe you will remember it in my wordless babble of contentment. Now, in leaving home I have come home. The babble is bodlondeb, contentment, the peace of being, the baby-labour, the building, the body being doubled.

Now it is sundered. It is what I am.